# TELL US WHEN TO GO

A NOVEL BY
EMIL DEANDREIS

Flexible Press
Minneapolis, Minnesota 2022

COPYRIGHT © 2022 Emil DeAndreis
All Rights Reserved. This is a work of fiction. Names, characters, places, and incidents either are the products of the author's imagination or are used fictitiously, and any resemblance to an actual person, living or dead, events, or locales is entirely coincidental.

Print ISBN: 978-1-7364033-8-9
eBook ISBN: 978-1-7364033-9-6

Flexible Press LLC
Editors William E Burleson
Vicki Adang, Mark My Words Editorial Services, LLC
Cover via Canva
Social media photos via Canva or by permission from Eric Ash, Mariann Bentz, Meghan Berry, Mark Bonsignore, William Burleson, Stephanie Crabtree, Kendall Deandreis, Anderson Giang, Ryan Hanlon, Larissa Horton, Dikshya Upreti, and the author.

## CONTENTS

APRIL 2007: ONCE UPON A TIME IN THE WEST 1

SEPTEMBER 2010: SAY YES 13

OCTOBER 2010: IN A HEARTBEAT 61

NOVEMBER 2010: A TIME FOR US 109

DECEMBER 2010: EASTERN PROMISES 181

JANUARY 2011: TELL ME WHEN TO GO 237

APRIL 2011: THE END IS THE BEGINNING IS THE END 243

For those at the whim of cities
that shift beneath them
like tectonic plates.

# APRIL 2007:
# ONCE UPON A TIME IN THE WEST

**Daryl Seager**

Just watched the MLB Draft. Couldn't help but think about Cole Gallegos. Has anyone seen him, at least? He's just a Kid y'all.

**Comments:**

> **Jayce Limerick**
>
> He sat in front of me in Macro Policy. He just stopped showing up one day mid-semester.
>
> **Greg Calderon**
>
> Shows him right. What happens when u run frm ur problems.
>
> **Liz Bunting**
>
> Greg is right. If he was my son… I would be Ashamed!!!

# ISAAC

## (1)

I REMEMBER WHEN Cole Gallegos decided to run away and take me with him. He was in my doorway, leaned up against it as if for support.

"Wanna come?" he asked.

He turned around back to his room, and I followed him there. I sat on his bed as he packed his boxes with perturbing inefficiency. Books thrown on top of unfolded shirts, topped with pillows. It took restraint to watch and not repack. Cole took down his posters. The "Impossible Is Nothing" one with Muhammad Ali looming over Sonny Liston. The 2006 Fresno State Baseball schedule with the blown-up picture of him, mid-pitch. It was odd to me why he hadn't taken that down months ago. Maybe he'd looked to it as a beacon of hope or was too throttled in his mind to even notice it there. His room was warm and sour, like there hadn't been many open doors lately.

"Where?" I asked.

"The City."

I would've guessed he'd say that. He always referred to his hometown, San Francisco, as The City, as if it was the only real one in a nation of imposters.

"And do what?"

He shrugged, likely already reaching his limit for questions about the future. "I dunno. Chill."

"They call that a lateral move," I said.

"Nice, college boy."

His insults had gotten faint over the semester, the way

sadness pales one's skin. Maybe he hadn't decided to run away yet but was gauging how the words felt to say. I probably could've given him some needed but generic advice like "stick it out, bro, at least finish your degree, you'll regret it later if you don't."

But I wasn't that type, which was part of why he kept me around when he'd closed out just about everyone else. Watching him the last three months had taught me how dismantled we can become in such a short time. There is always a threat to our mind, no matter how protected a fortress we may think it is. So I sat there on his bed considering his proposition, and I think he took solace in that. Filling our silence was the low hum of Wu Tang from his speakers, yet to be packed. Empty Gatorades everywhere, college carpet funk. The floorboards neighed in his back and forth from suitcases and cardboard boxes.

I'd been internship searching. Well, "searching." Which meant with zero instinct or urgency, typing words into Ask Jeeves and being confused by the results. I wasn't quite sure if this career immobility was a reflection of me, my Fresno State education, or the rotten US economy. I was only sure that the dude in front of me, Cole Gallegos, had improbably become my best friend over these last few years, and that held more magnetic pull than my many unknowns.

"Fuck it," I said.

## (2)

OUR FIRST CONVERSATION was back in '05 on the bus headed home from an exhibition against Bakersfield. This was when Cole was a freshman, bird-chested and jitter-less, always with a protein shake. A manufactured strut carried him around the weight room, a swagger he hadn't earned yet, but knew he would. His low nineties fastball was already gaining him clout on our team. He'd been granted passage to the back of the bus on trips, a place historically sequestered for upperclassmen. Matt Garza, whose face had most kids on the team too scared to talk to, picked up Cole from the dorms and took him to parties on the weekends.

I, on the other hand, was a DVD-on-Friday-night guy, forever waking up with my laptop on my lungs, the Start menu music on repeat. This left me something of a savant with movie scores. I could hear a shred of a song and tell you not just the movie, but the scene. *Schindler's List*, *The Sixth Sense*, *Matilda*, *Space Jam*, whatever. So many orchestral variations, teary piano numbers, waltzing through my mind at any moment as though accompaniment to my life.

So Cole wobbled up the aisle from the back where he'd been dipping with the seniors. As he sat down beside me, he caught his reflection in the bus window, shared a moment with himself, his nautical rope arms and surfer squint. I had my headphones on and was crocheting a scarf for a girl back home. She and I had always shared a thing for Harry Potter, had played "Hedwig's Theme" in orchestra together in high school. YouTube taught me how to crochet, my plan being to eventually announce my love for her with a Gryffindor scarf. As best I could, I'd tried to hide this from the baseball team and had, until this point, succeeded as a result of being mostly anonymous. But then here was Cole Gallegos sitting beside me with the spaghetti pile of yarn in my lap. He reached his arms for my head. I flinched, thinking he might pull me in for a headlock or pull some prank he'd been assigned by the seniors.

Instead, he lifted my headphones from my ears.

"Hey, Isaac," he said.

"Hey."

"Mind if I listen to your music?" he asked.

"All right."

He put the headphones on and then focused his eyes in

thought.

"What's this?"

"A soundtrack," I said.

"Which one?

"*Once Upon a Time in the West.*"

He slid the headphones back on and leaned back into the headrest, got comfortable.

"This is tight!" he said with the awkward force of people who don't know how loud they're talking. I couldn't tell if he was being real or a dick. "I feel like I heard this in a Jay-Z song." I smiled in a way that probably looked snobbish.

"Doubtful," I said.

"Eh," he weighed. He stood and left. No goodbye or nice talk. I was picking up my yarn and hook, thinking our exchange must have confirmed an assumption Cole had been concocting about me from afar, when he reappeared, this time with his iPod mini.

"Here," he said, then went scrolling his thumb in circles. "Listen."

As we drove past a wheaty expanse on I-5, my ears filled with Ennio Morricone, the gong and eerie chorus, conjuring visions of dusty pistol showdowns. Then there was the beat drop and a voice I assumed was Jay-Z's.

"Touché," I said.

"It's 'The Blueprint[2].' I listen to this shit before I pitch. This song makes me wanna, like, get in a bar fight. Doesn't it?"

In my silence, he looked disappointed, like if I had any other interpretation of the song than violence, it was dubious. I still hadn't ruled out that he wasn't fucking with me, carrying out some ritual to establish his dominance on the team, the way dudes single out other dudes in the prison yard.

"So what's that?" he asked.

I sighed.

"Crochet hook."

"That's a kind of knitting?"

"No."

I didn't know why I said that; it basically was knitting. I think I had my guard up, and I felt on some instinctive level that telling him he was wrong, even if he wasn't, preserved some leverage, some dignity.

"Oh," Cole said.

"I'm making a scarf. For a girl."

"Bold," he said. "How do you do that?"

I taught him what I could, and for the last leg of the trip, he asked me about the girl—peculiar questions like if she was a lake or ocean person—while making clumsy knots in the scarf, knots I was going to have to go back and fix later, but that was OK.

## (3)

COLE HIT HIS stride as a sophomore. What people thought he'd become, he became. It was a science, how his uniform gradually filled, and the stands filled as a result. He was clocked at 94 versus Boise State. When we got off the bus at UCLA and Cal State Fullerton, journalists snapped photos of him. This made him godlike on our team; even with his headphones on, asleep, he commanded our attention. He'd been spoken to by farm directors of a few MLB teams, who told him he was projected to go first round in next year's draft. "Don't knock a girl up," they said. "Monitor your social media. Be smart at parties. Everybody's got a camera now. Be a Jeter, not a Michael Phelps."

Cole ate it all up. The boos and shit talk from the frat bros of opposing schools; he put his hand to his ear, wanting more. Then he struck out the side and smiled up at the pedestrians that they were. A *Baseball America* article proclaimed Cole had the "It" factor.

Coach moved Cole out of the dorms and into the Arbor Place Apartments on North Tenth, where I lived with a couple other ballplayers. I think Coach wanted fewer distractions and temptations surrounding Cole, and someone like me—a frequent player of online Scrabble—made sense. Our pad had a couch in the living room with an Xbox and flat-screen, a couple of lawn chairs on the porch, the rusted bike of a past tenant. In the kitchen sink, dishes waited in an inch of gray water. At any given time, there were north of fifty unmatched ankle socks lying around, but other than that, our apartment was a fine incubator for a budding superstar.

With Cole's room across from mine, he liked to knock on my door if he heard noise coming from inside. Sometimes it was my guitar, and I showed him chords. One night I showed him the Jimi Hendrix chord. His attempts at "Purple Haze" were clunky and uncoordinated; to watch his face get all pinched in effort, to watch him fail at something, felt like behind-the-scenes access. He got into the habit of picking up the guitar by the neck, twisting his long fingers along the frets. He'd strum the Hendrix chord aimlessly, manifest some riff, and play it on a loop for thirty minutes. I think my room represented some portal to a world outside of baseball, outside of him. My dweeby disposition, indifference to winning or even competing, failure to think his fastball was the peak of human worth, and music and movie catalog: I was proof of such a world.

One night I was listening to the *Gladiator* soundtrack, and he stood from his chair in his room, walked across the hall to my doorway.

"Soundtrack," I said before he could ask.

"Don't act like you're busy. Soundtrack to what?"

"*Gladiator*."

He stood pensive in his sandals, dip in mouth. He let out a breath through his nose.

"It's perfect."

Cole downloaded the soundtrack. He'd been doing that a lot with my music, and that felt like a kind of validation. He skipped the emo stuff of my catalog, the Interpol and Modest Mouse and Death Cab, who he deemed whiners in need of a sexual encounter.

He listened to *Gladiator* in the pregame before his start against New Mexico and proceeded to throw a one-hit shutout. He sat mid-nineties in that Fresno afternoon air, hit 96 a handful of times. I counted eight scouts in Under Armour zip-ups with clipboards and stopwatches, all locked in on Cole. He went out that night to the bars and came back sometime after closing. I heard his heavy footfalls, accompanied by a lighter set of feet behind him. I was up watching *Eternal Sunshine*. My door flew open. His vodka smells reached me like the ripples from a recent boat. Cole walked up to me, held his fist out. I brought mine uncertainly to his. It was hard to see in the dark, but I could tell he was looking at me meaningfully.

"Right on," he said.

He turned out, back to his room.

"Oh, by the way, you got any music for sex?"

From Cole's room I heard two tiny thuds, what I assumed were girl shoes coming off.

"Good one," I said, but he'd already left.


Toward the end of my time at Fresno, it was no secret that I'd never had an official at bat. There was speculation on the team—mostly playful, sometimes not—over whether Coach even knew my name. Dudes asked me why I stuck it out, woke up for 6 a.m. weights, carried the helmets out to the field, threw batting practice and hit fungoes, only to hump the bench. I probably would have never considered it unless badgered, which I guess was evidence of my own blind spot. But my thoughts were, being anonymous on a roster gave me this insulated feeling, like a fish traveling in the middle of its school. Having a routine laid out for me—I found that comforting, given the alternative of figuring out who I actually was and what I wanted. That was what these numbnuts didn't understand: Baseball was just a placeholder until they were bitch-slapped very soon with the crisis of what to do with their lives.

When you looked at it that way, I wasn't that different than them. People outside the team were often surprised to learn I was on it, as though it defied their expectations that I wasn't a country music Neanderthal with a 2.0 GPA. But people didn't understand: fifty young dudes on a roster meant a mixed bag. Timid virgins. Rasta stoners. People who somehow could carry on a conversation about foreign policy. Some dudes would wind up rocket scientists, some gay, and sure, a lot of country music Neanderthals.

And yeah, me.


I still remember the morning a monarch butterfly fluttered into the batting cage. I was throwing batting practice. I wondered what the ping of the bat was like to the butterfly. Musical? Paralyzing? Or was it some undetectable sonar? It lofted to me in an unhurried flight. I tossed a pitch, and the ball went *vwam* past my ear. I realized that with all the netting, this butterfly probably wouldn't make it back out, so I cupped my hand around it, its bobby pin legs against my palm. Outside of the cage, the pitchers were just getting back from a jog, sitting down in their stretching circle, trickling ice water down their necks. I listened to them air obnoxious ideas. A relief pitcher named Doherty claimed STDs were a government scheme. The underclassmen looked around, went *pffff*.

When I opened my hands to free the butterfly, it stayed. My hand looked like some Impressionist painting. The pitchers stopped talking to give me incredulous glares, as if I could only be doing this to cement myself as alien to them. Cole wasn't looking at me but the butterfly, mid-butterfly stretch himself. He looked down at his knees, then back at the bug with a goofy smile, as though communicating, "We are one, little guy." The butterfly lifted off and shrunk into the blue morning. For a long time, I didn't understand what it was about that experience that stuck with me.

## (4)

COLE'S MELTDOWN CAME on quick. I barely had enough time to get used to this stuttering version of him before he was taking down his posters, asking me to go to San Francisco with him. I was a year older than him, had just graduated with a business degree, and didn't have a job lined up. What did I have better to do?

My parents supported my decision to accompany Cole. Though they were uneasy by my proximity to someone as unstable as Cole—as though he might be contagious—they admired my philanthropy. The recession was in its second year of making PhDs work at Starbucks. Even unpaid internships had applicants in their forties. The Escalades everyone had leased in the '05s and '06s? I wasn't seeing them hogging lanes as much. Laid-off men were hanging themselves in their defaulted houses. My dad couldn't tell me enough how barren the job market in my hometown, Riverside, had become.

"If and when the country figures a way out of its own grave, it's likely to start in the Bay Area," he said in response to my decision to move to San Francisco. His tone was tough to place—ambiguously grave? Whether he was encouraged or not by my decision to follow Cole to San Francisco, it seemed what mattered most was that his adult wisdoms were received by me as fact.

As much as I wanted to support Cole in dire times, I moved

to San Francisco to avoid moving home like every other college grad in America was doing. Sure, state school grads being unemployed right out of college wasn't unheard of. But Harvard, Stanford, and MIT grads were just as unemployed then. All across the country, parents were restructuring their basements into Welcome Home hovels for their millennial spawn, installing bathrooms, kitchenettes, sliding doors to the back yard. This was my nightmare. I cringed at the coddling I would endure: them asking me what I'd like them to stock the pantry with, them reminding me there was nothing to be ashamed of about moving home, us having little traditions like watching *Jeopardy* every night, them trying to not act hurt if I preferred to stay in my room. It would be sweet, don't get me wrong. But plenty of toxic things are sweet.

**SEPTEMBER 2010:
SAY YES**

# (5)

BY SEPTEMBER 2010, Cole and I had lived in San Francisco for two years without jobs. It was like those high school grad trips to Costa Rica or Paris, subsidized by parents, except this was ongoing and lacking fanfare. I was ashamed to take their money—I guess just a shade less than I would've been to move back home with them. On my laptop, I'd manicured a generic message and copied and pasted it to every job listing on Craigslist: barista, data entry, valet. I got used to the feeling of applying to jobs I was overqualified for and didn't want, and never hearing back.

Eventually, I was offered a group interview to sell knives. Applicants sat in a windowless room for two hours and watched a short woman demo the strength of their blades by slicing through leather wallets. She said, "When you show up on people's doorstep with this, they buy a set on the spot." None of the applicants was ever asked a question during the interview; we were all hired and congratulated with Safeway cookies. As we were leaving, they disclosed this job was commission only. Some kid raised his hand and asked what that meant. After explaining, the lady asked, "Is that going to be a problem?" The kid shook his head but looked frightened. My first day came; I no-showed.

Cole did the same thing for work—blasted emails to the furthest crevices of Craigslist—except he got fewer responses than I did because places really posed like you needed a bachelor's degree to fold their paninis for minimum wage. Cole, of course, had no such degree. It would be easy to determine that running away from college had been "short-sighted," but I would disagree. I'd seen him in Fresno in those final months, staring ghost-eyed at the back of a cereal box after sleepless nights, or staying in his room for so long I was certain it was empty, until I finally heard a toilet flush and then his door close behind him.

It was a terrible time to move anywhere in America or make a big decision or try to start any kind of life. Whatever stability you had, the feeling in the air was that you should cling to it, take no risks. Yet even in such a climate, Cole's decision to ditch his life had been correct in my estimation. And so here we were in this bone-chilling Sunset apartment, sitting on couches we'd found on the street, eating a lot of Tuna Helper, and we felt hopeless together, which was a kind of hope.

## (6)

HEADS OF SURFERS dotted the coast as we walked down the long hill toward Ocean Beach. On this late afternoon, the horizon was hazy like old Polaroids. Cole's sandals dragged their familiar sound, at one time a kind of strut of arrogance that had transitioned into a depression limp. He and I bought 32-ounce High Lifes at 45th and Vicente, close to the funk and rainbow spray of the ocean.

On the sand were picnics on blankets or tents to shield children from the sun. Dudes sat on driftwood drinking Fat Tire, this being the beer our generation chose to announce they were adults now. Cole and I clinked our jumbo bottles in the orange dusk. This was a celebration. We had both secured employment.

GO© was a Silicon Valley tech company—one of a notorious few—that was growing despite economic weariness. Their vision tickled the public and, recently, investors: a digitally mapped world. Their first offering a few years earlier had been satellite views of damn near everything. Even my mom knew about the feature. She liked to enter our address in GO©, zoom in all the way from outer space to our back yard, show guests, and say, "That's from before we resodded the lawn."

Now GO© was expanding to providing traffic data and directions. It was going to revolutionize transportation, make paper maps, and even printing directions from MapQuest, an endangered species. It never occurred to me to apply there; any company on the rise struck me as out of my league. But in their expansion, GO© was rapid-hiring temp workers for entry-level positions, which meant fresh college grads. Their headhunters probably filtered their search to all recent grads within a certain distance of their Mountain View headquarters, and then boom, I had an email from one of the Bay Area's fastest growing tech companies asking if I was interested in an interview.

Before the interview, I read that temp hires in America were up 25 percent in 2010, to nearly three million workers. Companies were mitigating the recession by hiring contract workers who could be paid less and fired easily. Which, of course, sounded scary. But I'd seen on social media a classmate from high school who was currently working as a temp for GO©. Her posts for the last six months did not suggest she was living in squalor or fear. A lot of yoga mats and cappuccino art. Selfies with bouncy hair at glimmering restaurants with hashtags like *#perks* and *#bestjobever*. I listed the girl as a reference when filling out my application, said she could speak to my problem-solving and team-leading skills. She definitely had no idea who I was.

When I called my dad and told him about the interview, he was eating something obnoxious like Corn Nuts. The rate of his chews conveyed his excitement. This was rare for him, excitement. He never showed it through words, but symptoms like this.

"Get a haircut. You look like that Goo Goo Dolls singer. It's unbecoming in a professional context."

I wanted to say, "Dad, I don't think that's how the world works anymore. People don't get denied employment on the basis of hair." But I knew he would say, "What the hell do you know about the world?"

And that would pretty much defeat me and every other millennial. We were entering a world we didn't know, little hatched turtles slapping at sand toward roaring, weird waves.

# (7)

THE DAY OF my interview, I walked through the lobby of GO© and watched a girl stop at an Odwalla refrigerator, help herself to one, and walk off. Odwalla had always been of a world just outside my reach, like paying for a massage or getting a full tank of gas. And here they were, casually free. The gravity of that was intimidating.

They put me in a room by myself for ten minutes. Colorful shapes hung from the ceiling. I sat on a rubber ball and observed posters, one of a Black girl playing hopscotch, and another for some French movie I'd never heard of. There was a foosball table in a corner, and in the middle of the room, a patch of grass with a spray bottle next to it. Was it a test?

My nerves burned when the door opened and the interview panel entered: two men, whose names I did not retain, one with a Bic-bald head, the other tall in plaid and vest. The third interviewer: a woman with short hair and Lego earrings, with what looked to be green Crocs. Audrey, chief communications officer, took a seat between the men. They placed four chilled Odwallas and a Rubik's Cube on the table, gave me their roles at the company and its spunky mission statement. Lacking bashfulness, Audrey detailed the recent wave of investors and the projections of GO©, particularly its maps division.

"But you're interviewing for this job, meaning you've

probably done your homework. So let's get into what matters. You. Isaac Moss. The worker, yes. But the person too. Are you a snug fit for GO©?"

Their relaxed smiles had a reverse effect, like they were gurus of concepts to which I was some grasping pupil.

"I could start with something like 'Tell me three words to describe you,' but that would be a little too Macy's for me. I worked at Macy's in high school. Ew. I think a more compelling entry point is your degree, Isaac. Fresno State. That right?"

"Yes."

"Our headhunters typically bring us grads from MIT, Stanford, Yale, and so forth. I wonder, how does your education from Fresno State set you apart from our typical applicants?"

This felt cutthroat, or perhaps that I felt this way made me fit the millennial stereotype. In my frozenness, the image of the girl in the lobby with the Odwalla popped into my mind. Simultaneously, one of my classes from FSU. Applied Business, a class stuffed with student athletes, taught by a poor professor who didn't have the stamina or personality to wall out the riffraff, so dudes just farted the minute he turned off the lights for PowerPoints. There was a lesson he taught once that stuck with me, a deflated outlook that imitated his demeanor, but here I was calling upon it in a time of desperation.

The lesson was: A job interview was nothing but floating ideas you couldn't believe you were saying, but with conviction.

"Sensitivity and oversight," I said.

Audrey nodded with furrowed eyebrows, Muppet-like. Had I intrigued or confused her?

"In Fresno," I continued, "I believe you see things up close."

Advice came back to me from a blog about interviewing for tech companies: *Because the questions can be cryptic, or deceptively basic, often the first answer or approach that enters your head is wrong.* But at this point, there was no turning back.

"Here at GO©, Odwalla is free," I said. "It was the first thing I noted walking through the lobby." I cleared my throat. The men on the panel nodded as though receiving anticipated praise.

"Perhaps to my Ivy League competition, this is standard, expected even. They drink one and toss it in the recycling. For those from lowly Fresno, however, Odwalla is a delicacy. I savor mouthfuls, swish them around. I read the words on the bottle, which tells me the bottle is plant-based and goes in compost, not recycling. I'm closer to the fruit pickers, the farmers, not the drinkers. If GO© is to have the global presence it aims for, it needs to value perspective like this. I comb the world at angles Ivy Leaguers might not."

Maybe that was cryptic enough, I thought, zested with a touch of condescension, to separate me from hundreds of other interviewees.

"Actually, Odwalla's bottles aren't biodegradable, despite being 'plant-based,'" Audrey said. "That's just a marketing ploy of theirs to win over consumers. Seems to be working. Good job by them! So if you see one of our employees put the bottle in recycling, they're doing the right thing. But I'm glad to see you comb the world at these angles, Isaac."

It occurred to me to leave the interview right then. But I was left no window, as Audrey tossed me a Rubik's Cube. At this, the men smiled, like it was some dorky checkmate.

"Comb this world," she said.

I exhaled, allowed myself to feel at peace with this entrapment, comforted perhaps that it couldn't get any worse. I felt my heart rate level, and I completed the cube in less than a minute and tossed it back. Thank you, high school statistics. The two men tilted their heads like small birds, and I thought I saw Audrey blush and peer at me differently. It made me attracted to her in a schoolyard-rivalry kind of way. I was asked other questions, some basic algorithmic questions, some longitudinal/latitudinal word problems, the logic of which was ferried to me by the dopamine of my Rubik's Cube performance.

Toward the end of the interview, I was having a daydream: Audrey and I, ten years down the road at our kitchen island, her hurrying to the shower saying, "I'm late, I'm late" as I eat Cinnamon Life, our son getting his face licked by our Bernese mountain dog, my favorite Elliot Smith song playing—"Say Yes" from *Good Will Hunting* when Will and Skylar have their first kiss, mouths full of burger.

One week later I was getting picked up on 19th Avenue, right outside the Sava Pool, by a bus with lavender LED lights and WiFi. It took me forty-five minutes south to GO© HQ for job training. I got a name tag, Isaac Moss. They gave me a badge that got me into the GO©-To Cafes and gyms and Namaste Nooks with massage chairs and Xboxes. After two years of Craigslist hunting, which was like being in a hallway where behind every door I opened was a brick wall, I finally had a job, an actual job, and it was for the fastest growing company in the Bay Area, with a lobby that looked like Chuck E. Cheese.

# COLE

## (8)

I CAME INTO a job this way, from an email forwarded to my Hotmail by my mom.

---

Subject: 49th?!?! WAS IT THIS BAD WHEN YOU WERE IN SCHOOL?

Hey Honey,
Janice just forwarded me this.
https://www.sfgate.com/education/article/Schools-students-sue-state-over-funding-3263839.php California schools rank 49th in the country, and SF district is the worst! Did you know about this? Sounds like teachers will go on strike soon. Or at the very least, many are moving to cities with higher wages and lower cost of living. If this happens, the district will need subs!
At least think about it? Love you,
Ma

---

My parents had started doing this more and more. Dropping what on first glance was an innocent thought, but beneath the surface was advice. I could feel my mom's strained breaths through my laptop, praying that I found my way. It had been two years of everyone trying to help without seeming like they were trying to help. I tried not to give off sullen vibes, but maybe that effort had its own stench.

Uncharacteristic of me, I clicked the article my boomer

mom had forwarded to me. I read what I'd heard others my age talking about on the bus, on the street, at parties to sound intelligent. San Francisco public schools were neck-deep in budget cuts. The latest was $113 mil, which meant hiring freezes across the district and swollen class sizes. And adjusted to cost of living, San Francisco Unified School District paid about the worst wages in the country. There were organized walkouts—parents extracting their children from school to march down Market Street, holding up signs that read, "Save Our Teachers, Save Our Schools, Save Our Futures."

I didn't get it. My memories of school were history lessons, values. Recess, rollerblading in MC Hammer pants around orange traffic cones. It struck me as such a protected institution, education. Not a place that could run out of money like a business goes bankrupt. And how was this happening in California of all places? All I ever heard was how California was so rich it could be its own country.

Something else I didn't get: What were my parents proposing I do, exactly? Apply for a job that had zero money to pay me? Not long ago I'd been widely considered the best college pitcher in the country, projected to sign in the first round for over a million dollars. Now, here were my parents and all their gray whispery friends urging me to be a substitute teacher. To join the haggards, the burnout hippies, the limpers, the leeches of federal money. The ones me and my friends fucked with in high school, treated like subhumans.

## (9)

WITHOUT A DEGREE, I was only eligible to be a substitute paraprofessional, which was a class aid who worked one on one with students in need of extra care. I remembered these ambiguous adults in my classes as a child, not fully understanding their role, not knowing their names. I'd observe them in the corner of the room doing things like clipping their fingernails.

The district processed my paperwork quicker than I wished, making me an official employee with an account and ID number. On the website I could peruse the different schools in need of substitute paraprofessionals. All around the city, from kindergarten through high school, were vacancies for me to select.

For my first day, I accepted a position at Sunrise Elementary School in the hills across from Mission Street. After checking into the main office and receiving a bathroom key, I was sent to the school's special day class, room 13.

"This is a Hate Free Zone!" read the laminated sign posted to the door of room 13. Next to it, icons of milk, peanuts, and wheat, all circled and crossed out. When I entered, a man twisted his body as though something important had escaped him.

"Dear, you frightened me," he said.

Something about "dear" made me feel blanketed.

"You must be filling in for Jenny today. Thank you for stepping in. Have you been to Sunrise Elementary before?"

"This is my first day," I said.

"At this school?"

"Nah, ever."

I must've given some confessional look.

"Aww, you big, scared puppy. You'll do great. The kids will be coming in any minute, so let's get you set up at the morning math station. Oh, and I'm Gary Truong."

I shook the man's hand; it was well moisturized, evidence of someone who had his life together.

I was becoming someone who more and more noted the habits of the normal. The people who did simple, smart things that it would never occur to me to do.

"What would you like the students to call you?" Gary asked.

"Cole."

"Mr. Cole? Or..."

It felt false to go by "mister." Like, people who ate cereal for dinner and did their laundry every three months were not to be Mister Anything.

"Well, to be real, they won't be calling you anything," Mr. Truong said nicely.

In the corner, a woman sang "The Wheels on the Bus" on a beanbag with a child on her lap. The woman clapped the girl's hands together, rocked and sang, and the girl's mouth moved. Off in another corner was a sink and a first-aid kit and a children's rug of foam puzzle pieces. On the board, there were photos of the students in the class, as well as the day's schedule in a rainbow of colors.

   7:55 Buses
   8:10 Breakfast
   8:25 Good Morning Circle
   8:45 Math
   9:20 Recess
   10:45 Snack
   11:00 Art
   11:30 Lunch
   12:30 Reading Circle
   1:00 Community Garden
   1:30 Choice Time
   2:00 Clean Up
   2:15 Goodbye Circle
   2:30 Buses

It had been years since I'd done so much by afternoon.

"This class has three students," Mr. Truong said. "Magda, Lupe, and Charles. They've got cognitive and developmental delay."

Mr. Truong sighed in thought.

"I think today we'll pair you up with Lupe. She's our little champion."

Mr. Truong then shadowboxed, I think. I wasn't sure what that meant.

"Lupe's mom drops her off a little late each day. She works three jobs. The last one ends at 4 a.m. at the Oakland Walmart, stocking shelves. Somewhere in there, she sleeps. Let's see. Things you need to know about Lupe. She will be sensitive to sudden noises. If she gets stung by a bee, she needs to be administered her EpiPen immediately. If for whatever reason she starts bleeding, we need to stop it, and then give her a helmet to wear for the rest of the day because she might pass out. She hates the helmet, so we put the sequins and feathers on it."

I didn't know what to say. What did one say in such conversations? Most of my life had been fastballs and burritos. Did I speak delicately given the subject, or just march matter-of-factly the way doctors shared news of terminal cancer and somehow slept after?

"The EpiPen can get stabbed anywhere?" I asked.

"Anywhere. Let's see, what else? Give her a graham cracker and she'll be your best friend for life. But keep them out of reach or they'll disappear. Avoid her pinches. Stronger than a crab's. Look."

Mr. Truong rolled up his sleeves, revealing a forearm that looked heroin-pocked.

"She'll swing at you too, so be on alert," he said. "She really loves hugs."

Lupe arrived. We sat in miniature chairs, and I followed her wandering eye. Lupe took out her communication board, where she could push buttons and it would cheerily sound "Bathroom!" "Snack!" "Take a break!"

"Are you excited for morning circle?" I asked, my voice

groggy. I felt a small, cold hand grab mine.

"She likes you!" Mr. Truong said, wrestling Charles's shoes on his feet. Charles proceeded to kick Mr. Truong in the nuts. Mr. Truong smiled and said, "No thank you!"

"Let's sort some socks, Lupe," I said.

"Snack!" she pressed.

"Look, red socks go with red socks."

She put a green with a red, then erupted into a laugh that got wheezy until, in moments, she was gasping for air. Over some socks. If I had to guess the last time I'd laughed that hard, it'd have to be *Jackass: The Movie*, seven years prior. That meant in Lupe's entire life I'd not laughed as hard as she was laughing.

"Those are Christmas colors," I said, holding up the two socks. "Do you like Christmas?"

I took a swift palm to my ear, a direct hit. My vision fuzzed. I'd always wondered if seeing stars was a thing, and it was, though if I were to describe it, it was more glittery.

"No thank you, Lupe!" Mr. Truong called from somewhere. "Quiet hands!"

Realistically, this was not language I could see myself adopting.

"Cole?" Mr. Truong called. "Lupe loves if you apply a little pressure when she's nervous, like this."

Mr. Truong scooted over and pumped Lupe's doll-sized shoulders, like one checks the air pressure of a basketball. Mr. Truong kneaded her neck, down her arms. Her eyes half-shut, her foot twitched.

"New environments, new people. It's difficult for her," Mr. Truong said.

In addition to the language, I was new to the concept of getting punched in the face and responding with compassion, which made me feel childish. I searched Lupe's face and thought I saw something, some awareness, like she knew the next time she threw a haymaker it would lead to a Swedish massage from Mr. Truong. Lupe yawned, as though to lull me, then sneakily raised a fist. I caught it mid-punch, held it, stared at her. She appeared amused, or impressed, like I'd passed a test.

"Heavens," Mr. Truong said after lunch. "I forgot about your break, Cole. Can you walk Charles to dance? And then take your fifteen? Make sure to hold tight. He's slippery."

I gripped Charles's squishy biceps and ferried him through the halls and dropped him off at dance, a room with colorful balls and a small trampoline. I didn't know where to spend my break.

Fifteen minutes was just long enough to begin to untense. Hunger had set in and hardened hours ago. I stepped into the faculty lounge, found two other paraprofessionals. One older woman with blue makeup sat on a plastic chair, massaging the balls of her feet. The other shaped her hand into a bird beak and pinched Chex Mix from a Ziploc. The microwave dinged a reminder. No one moved, just kept taking breaths that sounded like life support. I left that room, then the campus, and went across the street to a Greek delicatessen.

"The baba ganoush is very fresh," said the grocer. "Very creamy."

I passed the hip-high freezer with plastic containers and handwritten labels of orzo and dolma. The shelves held bottles of brandy with faded labels. In the aisles were old cans of SpaghettiOs and cat food. These were the kinds of stores that sold us booze on misty bonfire nights in high school. I felt a sadness for the clerk, who seemed to be bracing for rejection. I bought Nutter Butters, and the grocer accepted this decision with a solemn nod.

There were now ten minutes left on my break. I found myself in the empty schoolyard, where Mount Davidson and Sutro Tower loomed in the distance, their presence giving the air a particular quiet. I sat on the kids bench and felt the ache in my heels. I leaned forward, and the knuckles in my back obliged with pops. Halfway through this first day had me as physically taxed as pitching a complete game.

"Can you watch this young man while I run to the bathroom?"

A woman and child were next me, though I'd not seen them approaching.

"He likes to play catch," the woman said and underhanded me a tennis ball. "That will keep him more than busy."

The tennis ball was fresh from the tube with its smell of rubber and close-cropped fur.

Something in the boy's jolt upon sight of the ball reminded me of my Aunt Joyce's dog. Howard, the border collie, adored fetch and would ignore the world crumbling if someone was throwing him a ball. For many summers I was that someone.

Aunt Joyce's cabin was in Bend, Oregon, near Lake Trillium. My parents would send me up there for a week each summer. Family speculated that Aunt Joyce was a lesbian because, in her mid-thirties, she didn't have boyfriends and seemed to prefer dogs to humans. Her cabin had the smell of quilts and uncirculated air. I loved Howard, how he smiled outside the car windows and licked the food bowl across the floor.

On mornings, I sat outside, ate tablespoons of Jif, and petted Howard with my toes. I chopped firewood for Joyce's winter. Come afternoon, Howard got antsy and would bring a ball to me and herd me out of my chair. I took Howard to the nearby meadow and threw the ball.

My first few throws were always loopy and placid. Howard would promptly return with the ball, unimpressed. In time, I'd be tossing it a hundred yards across the meadow, and Howard would vanish in the reeds, the meadow going silent other than the staccato yacks of blue jays. Then there would be the rustle announcing Howard's return, foxtails and mustardy pollen on his eyelids. Eventually the ball would be puffy from spit. I'd wipe the slobber down my shorts. I loved watching that ball cut through the afternoon. I imagined the meadow having a consciousness, stretching its boundaries each day as my arm got stronger.

Before my senior year in high school, I came home from Joyce's cabin and went straight to an A's game, the KidZone where you can test your mphs. I paid the zitty worker, who gave me three balls. I hit 90 each time. Seeing that number on the radar gave me a Christmas-morning feeling. In bed at night, I indulged in baseball visions: pitching sequences in the bottom of the ninth, letting loose on a high 0-2 fastball, following that with a change-up outside, inducing a hopeless whiff. I romanced the all-night bus rides of the minor leagues, teammates snoring or playing cards. I pictured myself in a sports coat with hair gel and cologne, traveling on the team jet as a big leaguer, giving postgame interviews about how my arm got strong from Howard the dog. People would know me from this story, like how they knew Jerry Rice laid bricks before the NFL, which gave him his tough hands for end zone grabs, or how Dontrelle Willis honed his gangly delivery in the alleyways of Oakland, trying to strike out his friends. They would know me like that.

Growing up, I'd always heard adults refer to pro sports as silly, the idea that while most people played important roles in the functioning of society, overgrown boys got to stand around and slap asses for exponentially more money. But as a player, I'd never concurred. There had never been anything silly about facing a batter who stared at me like he'd choke me with his hands if he could. Nothing had been silly about the violence and precision of a slider low and away. But now that I was spending my day taking left hooks from a seven-year-old girl for $15 an hour, getting paid millions to throw a ball sounded really fucking silly. And enviable.

This kid was standing there Howard-like, awaiting my first toss. The ball left my fingers weird, like suddenly I had crab claws. It sailed over his head. He gave me a look, then joyfully bounded for the ball. Watching him gave me haunting memories of my catcher, Grubb, chasing down another wild pitch as disgruntled fans yelled, "Come on, Gallegos!" All those old sensations came back in an instant—the tight lungs, tunnel vision, hummingbird heart.

The boy returned, tossed a dart right at my chest, then beckoned, "Again!"

I'd lost feeling in my fingertips. I looked at the boy's chest, my target. How simple this game once was when the ball went to whatever I was looking at. My movement was now stiff and slow, like someone relearning motor skills after a car crash. I released the ball, and this time it skidded at the boy and bounced off his shins. He was delighted to chase after it again, his little jeans scissoring like a Lego figurine while I struggled for air.

"Thank you," the woman said when she returned. "How was he?"

She peered at me, then corrected her face and looked away as if I was deformed. I knew what I looked like. I'd seen the face in mirrors, splashing water on it after pitching. A shape of splotched, discolored putty. It was clear to her that in the minutes she'd been gone, something awful had happened.

"Did he misbehave?" she asked.

I wanted this moment done. I wanted it to have never been. This woman and her little ball-fiend boy, all erased. How easily the cosmos could have steered that woman toward another restroom or me to a different school or that little boy to an altogether different obsession than catch.

"This was my lunch break," I snapped, then put my head in

my hands. A curtain of chills lowered through me, leaving my thighs weak. "Fifteen minutes, in this whole day, that I had to myself." But she was already ushering the boy off. When I returned to Mr. Truong's room, Lupe was lifting the beanbag chair and heaving it into the soap dispenser.

"Welcome back!" Mr. Truong yelled as though a vacuum were on. His arms were protecting Charles and Magda as Lupe ran in a circle. She rushed to her table for a fistful of crayons and in a coloring book scrawled enormous spikes like a Richter scale of a devastating earthquake.

"Maybe I can help you color," I said to her softly.

She shouted no, gripped me by my ears, her eyes pleading. I placed my hands on her shoulder and squeezed like I'd been instructed. I saw my hand, reptilian in its dryness. My knuckles were a geometric marvel of creases, a feature of myself I had not noticed before. Lupe's eyes were drunk from my massage. We shared something with our eyes, an understanding, a tiredness. I would do this job only as long as I had to.

## (10)

I STARTED TO get numb to my phone ringing at 5 a.m., the automated call from the district listing the job vacancies for the day. My tendency was to ignore the call and silence my phone for a couple hours. When I woke back up, I would accept the job that was closest to me, steal whatever of Isaac's food I could without him noticing (a couple pieces of bread, a banana if there were more than two left), and head to the bus stop, or if the school was downhill, skateboard. I'd done this for two weeks now at various elementary and middle schools in the Sunset. It was funny the way the mind rationalized money. My first paycheck, a thousand and some change, felt like a fortune, simply because I was so used to having zero. Then I reminded myself how close I'd been to having one thousand times more money.

One morning, I took a job outside of the Sunset. I caught the 28 northbound on 19th Avenue and got off at Hennessey Field, where I'd played some of my games in high school. It was a wet morning, the water loud off passing tires. Brakes from MUNI whined and decompressed in a very San Francisco way. I passed a donut shop and looked at myself in the window—me and my old habits. Only these days, I looked not to admire myself, but to hopefully see something non-disappointing, like fashionably unkempt hair. I took notice of my baggy khakis: how they were stuck in the past, from the years when whatever size you were, you purchased three sizes bigger. This was the Limp Bizkit and frosted tips era, school dance mosh pit era, when I would jump and shove breathless to Blink-182 songs I didn't like.

Now in 2010, baggy seemed to be going extinct. I'd observed this in grown men who wore pants that were shrink-wrapped to their bruised-fruit-shaped asses, cuffs rolled tightly to the ankles, as if to imply wood chopping. All these non-gym-going dudes wearing skinny jeans and somehow having careers and joy. Yes, I was a bitter person, obviously. I'd have no problem admitting this to a psychiatrist, should I ever meet with one, and yes, I'd been recommended one many times. By my Coach Lonnie at Fresno State ("You know, these sports psychologists today understand athletes better than they understand themselves"), my dad ("People get paid a lot of money to help others. They're professional, and they wouldn't be employed if what they did didn't work"), girls who hardly knew me ("Therapy, like, saves lives"). Not to mention all the posts I would snoop on sleepless nights, back when social media was new and clumsy and people said things not knowing everyone could see ("Zoloft, Xanax, Prozac! Try something! This is getting too hard to watch am I right?!").

Yips. It had a name, and a very insufficient definition, and nothing else. Yet everyone was apparently an expert. I was not morally averse to therapy. I guess part of my disease was my certainty that it wouldn't work.

I tugged the pant legs of my khakis up, felt the wet ends bite my ankle. There was logic to why I was wearing these busted-ass pants. I'd worked ten days as a substitute paraprofessional thus far, and after each one, I'd gone home with stained or ripped clothes. Being a paraprofessional meant providing for children who had special needs and shifting moods and limited means of communicating them. And at times, it had proven to be a paper towel commercial. Today I'd accepted my first high school assignment with no idea what that entailed. So, not that I had any nice pants, but if I did, I wasn't wearing them to work.

I signed the visitor binder in the main office of Seaside High and received a copy of the bell schedule and a bathroom key from the assistant. On my way out, I paused at a glass jar of candy. If there was a list of people this candy was intended for, I didn't feel a sub para was on it. The nature of a sub was not belonging anywhere. Whatever. I took a handful of bite-sized Three Musketeers anyway and hoped no one noticed.

Wedged between a 10-A Storage and 10-C Incinerator, I nearly missed my assigned room, 10-B. Inside was a stout man leaning against a stool, maybe mid-thirties, in a polo and jeans. He looked at me in the doorway and laughed.

"Welp, looks like Theo did quit. Come on in, man. I'm Mr. Antonini."

"Cole."

"And what do you go by with the students?"

All teachers did this. It was more a gesture of professionalism, it seemed. The reality was, no students cared enough to learn my name, and I would never see them again once the day ended. Mostly, kids looked right through me, which if I was being honest, I preferred. "Cole works."

"So Cole, right now, we're rockin' a thin crowd. Typical Monday. Over there we've got Grayson, fresh out of Mom's

RAV4."

Grayson turned to me.

"One hundred and seven thousand miles, cobalt blue," he said seriously.

"Grayson cruises in everyday from Antioch," Mr. Antonini said.

"I wake up at four!"

Grayson shifted in a way that revealed one of his arms was shorter than the other.

"What car did you drive to school?" he asked.

"I took the bus."

"Oh," Grayson said sadly.

The other student in the class scoffed with a "psh."

"That one right there is O'Shea," Mr. Antonini said. "O'Shea, you wanna say anything about yourself? How about what you did this weekend?"

"No."

"Too cool. Let's see. Lemme fill you in then. He rides pink rollerblades to school. He's prolly rocking out to Justin Bieber right now. I miss anything?"

"This man so square, bruh." O'Shea scrolled his thumb across his phone.

"Anyway, these are the two. We got a few more. I say for now, Cole? Enjoy the quiet."

"Totally," Grayson said, then walked over to the metal turnstile bookshelf, depleted of books, and chose a *Clifford*.

I sat beside Grayson and zoned out at a stain on the wall. As a kid, I used to take note of when people did that. An old man on a train, a tired mom scanning groceries, a teacher at her desk while her students worked independently; I'd catch people in a moment, their eyes eerily distant, their faces showing neither crisis nor contentment. I would assume they were having some sobering epiphany, like, "So this is my life?" Not wanting to ever look like them, I had this thing where if I were ever lost in thought, I would try to appear in the midst of some thrilling thought. But now, staring blankly at the wall, I knew what I looked like, and there was no fight in me to be otherwise.

"Isn't it your birthday, Grayson?" Mr. Antonini asked. Grayson crossed his arms and closed his eyes regally. "Happy birthday, old man!" he said.

"After school my mom is taking me to Panda Express, and she's getting me a video game."

"When everybody's here, we'll sing happy birthday," Mr. Antonini said.

"What video game you finna get?" O'Shea asked.

"*Call of Duty: Black Ops* or *Assassin's Creed: Brotherhood*."

"You ain't got *Black Ops* yet?"

Grayson straightened his posture and didn't confirm or deny.

"I be gettin' bodies in *Black Ops*," O'Shea said.

The door closed. Standing inside was a new boy, brushing his hair forward with a handleless brush.

"Top of the morning, Delfino," Mr. Antonini said.

"Good morning, crack baby," O'Shea said.

"O'Shea, why the hostility? Delfino is your friend," Mr. Antonini said.

"Little squeaky bitch ass mama boy," Delfino said.

"You get a fade?" O'Shea asked him.

"Yeah."

"Where?"

"My cousin house."

O'Shea made a doubtful face. Delfino worked the brush. It sounded like a patio being swept in the distance.

"Sometimes it takes me three hours to get home," Grayson said unprompted. "Because of the bridge. My mom puts on KMEL or sometimes the God channel."

"Why do you go here if you live so far?" I asked.

"'Cause I just moved there 'cause we were living here with

my uncle but he got laid off and then my mom couldn't afford it here either so we just moved to my other uncle's. I didn't wanna switch schools for just one year 'cause of my friends."

I noticed Delfino and O'Shea closer to each other, appearing to smell each other.

"Boys. Come on, it's *Monday*," Mr. Antonini said.

"Lil Herbal Essences bitch, you ain't about this life," Delfino said, standing tall in his blue windbreaker and bleach-washed jeans, a dime-sized gray spot above his right ear like a storm on a planet. Arms were firm by his side.

"Why yo eyes so far apart like Shrek?" O'Shea said at Delfino.

Delfino put his bent elbow against O'Shea's throat, sneakers squeaking, desks falling sideways and jamming against one another. Delfino and O'Shea scooted back from each other ram-like, getting their footing, asses out.

"Time for math packets!" Mr. Antonini cried.

Delfino's arms whiffed. O'Shea bobbed, pendulous until Delfino connected on his upper cheek. I was unnerved by the click. O'Shea crowd-surfed across chairs. Then two security guards appeared in the doorway. The boys took this as an opportunity to catch their breath.

"You ain't got rounds in you, lil delicate ass," Delfino said.

He sucked in his nose. O'Shea blinked and shrugged like he was bored. Both left without complaint

"We're actually not supposed to intervene," Mr. Antonini said eventually, breaking the silence. "Something about how a teacher cracked his skull trying to stop a fight and there was lawsuit stuff. So now when the fights happen, we're just supposed to go to the hall and flag down a security guard like a cab. That's why I stood there, during that. In case you were wondering. I'm not saying it's gonna happen again today, but you never know. And if they do go at it, just don't get in the middle, unless one of them is, you know."

"What a system," I said.

"Right?" Mr. Antonini said.

"That's like restaurants throwing out food instead of giving it to the hungry, just so they don't get sued."

That was my follow-up. In the flash that the idea was in the chamber, it sounded sensible, even clever. It was the kind of thing I could try out on Isaac. If it ended up dumb, there were no consequences, other than a sharp Isaac quip. But now I felt the searing heat of releasing a thought or opinion in the real world. Mr. Antonini nodded, then his nod slowed, and he looked up, as if detecting an odd smell.

"Administration's gonna fill out incident reports. Then there's conflict mediation, a kind of restorative justice. The boys go in a room and are supposed to talk it out. Schools around here had the right idea a while back to have students facilitate this instead of adults. Because with adults, it feels all paperworky and the kids don't even tell the truth because of a code among each other. So it's got a lot of potential. But right now I know it's just their buddies, and they go back in a room and knock out a couple *Chappelle's Shows*."

He cleared his throat.

"At any rate. Listen. Now's probably a good time to take a little break. The others—they usually make their way to class, oh..."

He looked at the clock hanging by its cord from the wall, angled at the floor, a dead sunflower ticking.

"Soon."

# (11)

I LEFT CAMPUS and found myself on Van Ness, the potholed road that sliced diagonal through the city. On it was a Porsche dealership, the opera house, and homelessness. On Van Ness was also Tommy's Joynt, the meat-and-sides place where the

University of San Francisco took me on my first recruitment lunch back in high school, when my career was puppy young with easy thrills. It had only been five years since then, but lately it all felt so distant that I might need convincing that it ever happened at all.

USF had watched me pitch a foggy game in Pacifica, asked if I'd like to get lunch sometime. This being my first recruitment lunch, I told myself not to say the wrong thing. No swear words—these guys were Catholics. At that point, I had a vague understanding that I was good at baseball but didn't know how good. I'd just spent the summer eating peanut butter and playing fetch with a dog, and suddenly my toes were splitting my shoes and I was grooving low nineties.

Above our booth at Tommy's Joynt was a black-and-white photo of old San Francisco, 1850s Market Street, with a wood plank Wells Fargo sign and a horse-drawn carriage on a dirt road. I observed how the head and assistant coaches uncocooned the napkins from their silverware and laid them in their laps. I did the same, and as I did, saw a man at the counter in a black overcoat and combed black hair, as though he were Dracula himself ordering a to-go pint of blood. Then he walked with his plate over to our table and sat down. It was the mayor of San Francisco.

"Gavin Newsom and I go back a ways," USF's head coach said. "He pitched for Santa Clara, but we won't hold that against him. I asked him to be here today to talk about what it means to be a hometown hero. I hope you don't mind him joining."

I tried to project calmness, as if this was expected, though I had a hunch that USF didn't call in favors like this for all their recruits. Mayor Newsom sent hints that were both inspiring and nondescript that I had the makings of a San Francisco legend.

"I'm told you're in the low nineties now," Mayor Newsom said. "And you've got the shoulders of someone who could keep throwing harder. But to me what's more intriguing is what these gentlemen say they see in your disposition, and eyes. Like you walk around with a bullet-proof vest."

He seesawed prime rib.

"That's what places you in a different category. And the city needs that kind of character and pedigree repping it."

The feeling I had in that moment was what I imagined superheroes felt just before soaring above skylines to fight evil. It made the act of smoothly forking food impossible.

The mayor checked his watch and dabbed the sides of his mouth with his napkin. It was clear that his part of the lunch was over. He shook my hand, made some closing remarks with words like "integrity." I pressed for any sophisticated questions I could ask to prolong this moment.

When it was back to the three of us, the coaches saw my eyes and flushed cheeks and nodded as in, *yeah, kid, that just happened.*

Word spread about me, and soon I was coming home from school to a stack of recruitment mail, everywhere from liberal arts D3s to bona fide D1s. A month after my lunch with USF, I was picked up at San Diego International Airport by Tony Gwynn, head coach of SDSU. Not the assistant coach or the media operations intern, but Gwynn himself, flashing his caution lights in arrivals. His stature was generous in his SUV; I didn't dare rest my elbow on the center console. For this trip I'd made sure to tuck in my shirt, which always embarrassed me, how it made me look church-going and lame. I wasn't sure if Tony was the type to value such a gesture or resent the pretense. So it felt like a risk either way.

"I brought your rookie card," I said in the car. "I hope you'll sign it." Tony smiled the way he might dismiss a dweeby journalist. "It seems like you got your three-thousandth hit yesterday."

I could tell Tony's objective was not to romance his career or use it as a recruitment tool, but I couldn't help but get these things off my chest. It felt artificial to sit there with Tony Gwynn and pretend I was interested in a school's majors, facilities, and dormitories.

"Heck, sometimes I still wake up and reach for my stirrups," he said, and that was that.

He chewed gum that was as pink as a hippo's mouth. Of all the coaches I'd met, Gwynn demonstrated the most comprehensive plan for me. There was no rhetoric. He didn't try to seduce me with *nudge nudge, wink wink* talk of sorority girls like the coaches at UNLV and Arizona State had. In the moment, those advertisements had tantalized, but they aged poorly in my mind. Tony spoke plainly, undesperately; it refreshed me.

"We need a Friday night guy for three years. After that, you'll get drafted. We'll getcha set up with Boras. That's how this thing will shake out. In those three years you're here, we're not talking about conference titles. We're talking about the whole dang thing."

The sky was swerving orange. I thought I tasted the fizz of the surf from somewhere.

"We've got a verbal commit from a kid a year younger than you. Local kid. He's been overlooked because he's had some weight issues."

Tony paused, gave a playful glance for the irony.

"His name's Stephen Strasburg. With you both on the team, I could see people talking about y'all the way they still talk about Will Clark and Raphael Palmeiro. That's big-time vocabulary."

He knew I was an SF kid, that I'd probably spent my childhood practicing Will Clark's swing in the mirror.

"How about let's get some ice cream?" Tony asked.

Gwynn was catcalled from passing cars as we walked, his flip-flops slapping his heels. Grains of sand crunched. The waves got louder, the salt and Snoop Dogg in the air, the high sidewalk curbs that I associated with southern California. It was in the low seventies, an occasional breeze coaxing noise from palm trees.

"About right now—have a look around, take a breath—this is when you'd be throwing first pitch," Gwynn said.

"It's beautiful, Coach."

I did some arm circles, perhaps a nervous tic, like our silence needed movement. Gwynn watched plainly. Then he held his ice-cream cone like the handle of a bat, left hand on top of right. On the sidewalk, in khaki shorts, Gwynn sunk into his Hall of Fame stance. I did what I guessed was the logical next thing, a mock pitching delivery, loose coins jingling in my pocket. Gwynn mimicked his swing; what little ice cream remained stayed hunkered in the cone. We stood under the night's first stars, on what was essentially a middle school date between me and Tony Gwynn.

This stuff was happening too quick to fathom. I mean, I was still putting Noxzema on my neck pimples, still getting driven to games in the family van with Costco juice boxes in the back. Yet suddenly I was worth over $100k in the minds of NCAA coaches. I was a red-carpet celebrity in this niche world of college baseball.

Come spring, coaches from all over were at my games. Sometimes I found them unhalving their flip phones in boredom or chatting among themselves for full innings without watching a pitch. Which meant they'd seen what they needed to and could now report to whoever they reported to: The hype on this kid was real.

In the end, I chose Fresno State. It was in a flat region of lemon orchards, taquito wrappers, and meth. *Baseball America* ran a piece on my decision. In my interview, I said I wanted to play for a team in a place that could use a hero. People on blogs were perplexed and doubtful. They thought there was more there, some irregularity of the mind, a strange ego, or fear of the big stage, though a diagnosis no one was brazen enough to give. Just that it didn't bode well. Back then, the doubt motivated me, made me better. But eventually those bastards turned out to be right.

"Baseball, man," Gwynn said in the bruising night, on a recruitment trip that would yield a full ride offer that I'd decline. "Baseball." And that captured everything.

# (12)

MR. ANTONINI GAVE me the sense that my break window was a little looser than at other schools, so I meandered down Van Ness. I read menus taped to windows. A corner store counter had a protective cage of metal wire and a TV showing security footage from six different areas. I walked down a narrow aisle of Spam and boxed Fanta. At the refrigerator, I marinated on the forties. All those cold high school nights in Golden Gate Park, wiping runny noses, worrying about cops, chopping it up with homeless, giving them swigs. I grabbed string cheese out of the fridge, passed the porn and the Hostess on my way to the counter. The clerk was trim in a white V-neck with a jade pendant. He eyed my item, then punched a number into the register.

"Two twenty-five."

"For a string cheese?"

He turned to his soap operas. These were moments that felt like the world was edging me out, per some script written for my life. Did I bring things onto myself in ways I was unaware of, on the baseball field and off? I felt compelled, for lack of anything else pressing in this moment, to confront this rather than let the feeling of it spread through me and eat at me the rest of the day. But before I could, the clerk shouted, "No!"

"No what?" I asked.

"Get out of the store!"

I touched my chest, then throat. Had I said something? Was that how these self-advocacy moments happened—out of body?

"*Get out of the store,*" a girl said in a mocking voice behind me. "Shut up, you lil ass rat."

Two girls danced down the aisle, arm in arm, the shorter one in a leather jacket being led by the taller one with fluffed amber hair.

"I will shop in this establishment," the taller girl sang.

The clerk consulted his security screen, watched their images consider potato chips.

"They never pay," he confided. The girls returned to the counter.

"Don't look at me like that," the taller girl said.

The cashier grimaced like he was being forced to go into business with people who'd slain his family. He punched a number.

"Fifteen ninety-nine."

"This—*wow*. This man just said fifteen dollars?" said the shorter girl.

The girls looked at one another, steamed but not without excitement.

"Y'all people supposed to be good at numbers. It's ninety-nine cents for Arizona—you could see right here on the can, retard. I got some Mambas. How you about to say fifteen dollars for juice and candy?" said the tall girl.

"Like, we trying to pay you. Turtle face," said the shorter one.

"This dude irritate me. He really lucky he behind that chicken cage."

"Nobody gon tell me I can't eat. Period."

"Dizzy, get some Cup Noodles while we at it if he gonna play games. Shit."

The taller girl, Dizzy, sprung into a pirouette in Jordans,

and then on her toes flipped off the camera.

"The fuck you lookin' at in yo dad pants?" Dizzy shot at me.

Stunned, I glimpsed my khakis. I had an urge, residual from my earlier near standoff, to come back at this girl, this stranger, something like, "I know these pants suck and am only wearing them because..." but that would be insane. Whatever I responded, she'd probably clap back with something way more hurtful, or just punch me. Before I could do anything, they bulldozed me into the Cheetos.

"Stop them!" the clerk cried. He rushed to his little cage door and jingled his keys. His whole situation rattled, and by the time he opened the door, the girls had disappeared into the morning.

# (13)

WHEN I RETURNED to 10-B, Dizzy and her friend from the store were there. Dizzy looked at me plainly, as though having no recollection that moments before she'd sacked me.

"Cole, would you mind helping Dizzy get on task? She's just arrived to school. We're reading *House on Mango Street*, and she's working on her vocabulary packet. Dizzy, meet Cole, our helper for the day."

"Mr. Antonini, I know you didn't just send this plumber to sit wit me," Dizzy said.

"Bitch said plumber," her friend said, laughing.

Dizzy's hands were spread across the vocabulary packet like she was trying to hide something. She had a tight-wound neck inside her black North Face jacket. Her freckles were carrot colored, her eyebrows Band-Aid wide.

"I'm Cole."

I pulled up a chair, and it honked across the floor. Dizzy mugged me as if the noise was symbolic of my whole being.

And my name surely confirmed this for her. Cole. A flimsy white name. The official name of Dad Pants. What even was my name, Cole Gallegos? A hypocrisy, a paradox. A great-grandpa immigrated from Mexico, the city I was never told, almost a hundred years before. I was a fourth-generation San Franciscan. I didn't feel a part of any cultural heritage beyond the Sunset District, the dim sum and Irish pubs and surf vagabonds of Noriega. I didn't know Spanish despite wavy hair and tan, which made dudes in taquerias address me in Spanish, leaving me to slump and mutter "black beans." It was understandable if Dizzy never believed I was a superstar in this city.

"Yo breath smell like dick," she said.

"OK."

She probably had a point. I'd just eaten cheese and could taste the sourness in my mouth. Her mind worked like a good fastball, sneaky and accurate. She snapped a number two pencil in half.

"I need a new pencil."

I noticed her fingernails were bitten down to the pink tips. "I bite my nails too," I said, an attempt at something.

"Grayson, lemme see yo vocab packet," Dizzy said.

"Let Grayson work independently, please," Mr. Antonini said.

"Nobody gonna ignore me. Grayson!"

"Bitch, shut up," O'Shea said from across the room.

"Nobody talking to you wit yo pruny elbows. You need Crisco. And I don't even know why you talking when Delfino cracked yo shit earlier."

"Never that."

"Psh. You was cracked."

"Delfino a peasant."

"Watch me whomp yo malnourished ass again," Delfino said contently.

"I don't give a fuck," O'Shea said. Delfino turned back

around in his chair. Somehow this wound up feeling like an amicable exchange.

"Grayson. Look at me. You being rude," Dizzy said.

Grayson kept his eyes down on his paper, which I thought might be some survival instinct, a form of playing dead for fear of becoming prey.

"Dizzy, people are trying to learn," Mr. Antonini said.

"Ain't nobody trying to learn shit."

"Dizzy."

"I'm tryin' to learn, but it's retards in here, Grayson. When we got retarded people, it interfere wit my education."

"Nobody in this class is retarded. Not Grayson, not you," Mr. Antonini said.

"Grayson retarded."

"I really wish you wouldn't use that word, speaking of vocabulary."

My blood felt warmer, and my teeth were clamping down, making a tightness in my temple.

"Let's do the next word," Mr. Antonini said.

"Fuc...Fuc...Fuck sha," Grayson said.

"Fuchsia," Mr. Antonini said. "That's a tough one."

"I ain't doin' this fuckin' vocab packet, Mr. Antonini," Dizzy said. "You out here havin' us define *tamale*. Stop."

She stood.

"Where are you going?" Mr. Antonini asked.

"Bathroom."

Mr. Antonini put his head in his hands. "You just got to school."

"How you bout to tell me I can't?"

I noticed a security guard in the corner of the room, who must have quietly stuck around after escorting Delfino and O'Shea back to class post-fight. He didn't look like the security guards one might imagine: arms folded, broad, and surly. Rather, he was hunched and mouse-eyed, as though waiting to be told what to do.

"Move," Dizzy told him.

"No," the guard stammered.

"Why do everyone be so agitating today?"

She unzipped her jacket and threw it onto her chair, then clasped the guard's hands and pressed them against her chest. He wriggled and tugged, but clearly stronger than him, she had him hopelessly locked to her. She pushed so hard her chest dimpled like parentheses. She rubbed his hands in car wax circles. His face was quickly aglow.

"Security guard nasty!" Dizzy yelled. "*Rape!*"

She let go of him, and the force of his resistance sent him careening backward into the wall. Dizzy was gone.

At lunch, I was on supervision with Grayson. In a shaded corner, skaters played Beastie Boys from an old boom box. The thwack of ollies ricocheted. The football team sat on top of tables, elbows on knees in their game-day white jerseys, eating cafeteria lunch. One of them, tall and lanky with designs in his hair, tossed an orange into a huddle of freshmen, who shrieked. My phone vibrated, a text from Isaac.

> You ever had acai?

I replied,

> Def not... Good?

Grayson scratched his head in a daze.

"Do you know Barry Bonds' batting average in the 2002 World Series?" he asked.

"I do not," I said. I could've told the truth, which was that I'd gone to Game 3 and knew everything there was to know about that World Series, but despite liking Grayson, I could no longer tolerate baseball as a topic of small talk.

".471. With four homers," Grayson gloated.

"What's your favorite food?" I asked, a hope to steer the conversation.

"Hot Pockets. Do you know my favorite baseball player of now-times is? Tim Lincecum. I have his autograph from Fan Day. My mom parked at the pier, and we had to walk. I weigh more than him by twenty-eight pounds. He eats at In-N-Out. He got caught smoking marijuana by the police. He won the Cy Young Award for two years."

I felt dread that if this conversation kept going, it would go through all current baseball players until it arrived at almost-baseball players like me, and somehow he'd know all the stats of my career: Cole Gallegos had 236 strikeouts his freshman year and zero his senior year.

"Let's talk about your favorite movie, Grayson."

"*Iron Man 2*. Buster Posey is my second favorite baseball player. He's hitting .300. He might win Rookie of the Year. The Giants have Cy Youngs and Rookies of the Year! Did you know that Jonathan Sanchez threw a no-hitter last year?"

"I did," I said, putting my hands in my pockets. Isaac had replied:

Undecided…

"Did you know it would have been a perfect game?" Grayson asked. "A perfect game! If it wasn't for one little thing."

Riveting

I texted back.

I'd had an almost-perfect game once, and the "one little thing" that doused it. The one little thing wound up being the biggest of things. The thing I still can't shake. A mistake? Lapse of focus? Evidence of higher power?

It was a warm April night, humid, sophomore year. I got through the seventh inning—twenty-one outs—without allowing a base runner. The crowd's buzz told me they were aware of the gravity of this development. On my way back to the dugout, I let myself look up into the crowd, just a glance. Cameras aimed at me from the *Fresno Bee*, dads pointing the attention of their boys at me, lip-glossed girls. I was amused at how attraction worked: Because I was better at throwing a ball than this team was at swinging a bat, I was going to get laid tonight, when really, what was sexy about a pitcher? Tight pants, sure. Swagger, OK. But no doubt, aliens were watching the fanfare over me going *huh*?

The ninth inning came—perfect game intact. The crowd was on its feet. I heard the roars from the dugout, my boys wound tightly for the impending celebration like an inching champagne cork. After warm-ups, the catcher threw down, infield went around the horn. Third baseman underhanded it to me, didn't give me any wink, no meaningful nod. It was kind of a silent pledge: I will do my job, this is your show. Like a good worker bee, I thought. I appreciated baseball's unspoken understandings, the sensitive chemistry and ritual in these moments, like how no one had spoken to me since the fifth inning. This was the hierarchy. When I pitched, they knew to be on their game. This power was intoxicating.

I grooved a hip-high first pitch, caught the zone. The second pitch, a touch higher. The batter took the bait, flew out to the catcher. Easy first out. The second out was even easier. First pitch down the middle, the batter clearly taking all the way. I never understood that strategy: making the pitcher throw you a strike when you're losing in the ninth. The idea was to make the pitcher work, put the pressure on him, but the way I saw it was, you're losing, the pressure is on you. Why give the guy with the advantage more of an advantage? I flipped an easy slider that made the batter look stupid. Then, 0-2, I yanked another slider harder and farther down in the zone. The batter check-swung too far. Two outs. One away from perfection.

The next batter fell down 0-2 quick, then fouled off two fastballs and spit on two sliders in the dirt. Suddenly things were interesting. I looked into my catcher, Grubb, who looked into the dugout—the chain of command for calling pitches. It was standard for the signs to get more cryptic in later innings, college coaches being forever paranoid of picked signs. Grubb tapped his chest and knee, performing an exhaustive charade of Morse code. It was a curveball, I determined. Or was it?

I swore it was. But this was no time to be unsure of a pitch call. I stepped off the rubber. The batter relaxed his hands, the umpire stood out of his crouch. Out in left field, I heard the pops of the bullpen getting hot. It was Gilmore or Gutierrez or Wartman, probably, though all that could be seen was the color of bodies blinking through the fence. They were out there just in case I coughed up a hit and things escalated quickly; we were only up by two. The scoreboard read ninety-eight pitches, my season high.

My shoulder felt a little heavy, nothing I hadn't felt before.

Had Coach really called a curve, though? A 2-2 count, this late in a game, perfect game on the line? Was this Coach's way of showing faith in the curve or doubt in the fastball? The PA filled the silence with a sound bite.

*Ev-ery-body-clap-your-hands!*

The hands of the crowd were sharp, a sound akin to the thwack of a wood bat. Romantic, really. The batter stepped back into the box. Judging from his hyper little batting stance, this kid was the type who did all the little things coaches loved, like running hard nineties, laying down great bunts, diving for everything even if it was out of reach. I wanted to drill dudes like that in the back. But I couldn't. Not tonight, one strike from perfection, media coverage, higher draft pick, higher signing bonus.

I edged my heels back on the mound, motioned for the sign again. Left knee, right knee, mask, chest, mask, right knee. Indeed it was a curve. I didn't shake off; bad juju to do that, to act bigger than your role and tempt the gods. I let my shoulders slack, relaxed my glove at my belt, found the curve grip. This was a still moment, a morning lake yet to be rippled. I let out a breath, then drove to the plate. I tugged down on the ball, but got under it just a bit because my forearms were toast. The curve started high, needed to bite soon. The batter dropped his shoulder and tried to wear it, tried to end the perfect game by getting nicked by a curve, which was so something this type of kid would do. The ball was caught inside. Ball three. Full count.

Coach didn't even call a sign. Fastball all the way.

My thoughts: Had anyone from Fresno State ever thrown a perfect game, and how much would this perfect game improve my projections in the draft? I began my windup. Maybe I should have taken my time, let out another breath or two, flushed those thoughts of the future. Mid-delivery I became aware of the intricacies of the baseball seams. Why did I do that, with everything riding on this moment? Have some simple stoner epiphany. Then it was time to release. My entire life, how many pitches had I thrown? Thousands. Tens of thousands even. Not once had I ever been thinking about the ball at the moment of release. What a great irony it was that now, amid the most important pitch of my life, I changed what worked.

The ball left my hand and was immediately unmappable. Grubb didn't move. Nor the batter. The ball seethed over the press box and clear out of the stadium. It was really gone before I ever had a chance to see it move, doubtable like a shooting star. Then, to establish this had not been imagined, car alarms started going off in the parking lot.

Ball four.

With nobody on base, it didn't even go down as a wild pitch.

In essence, the pitch hadn't ever really happened. The phenomenon of it was not recordable in baseball. It would exist in the future only as folklore. To everyone but me. The umpire threw out a new ball. Right when the game resumed, Grubb picked the idiot runner off first for the third out. Perfect game gone, no-hitter complete. The celebration on the mound was eerie; guys stood out there like they were at a party where they didn't know anyone.

I could hardly understand my achievement, if that was how it was to be remembered. I spent hours at home that night trying to get into my mind and re-feel the sensations at the moment of the throw, obtain the flight recorder of my combustion. Those hours spilled into the next morning, which spilled into months, which became years.

# (14)

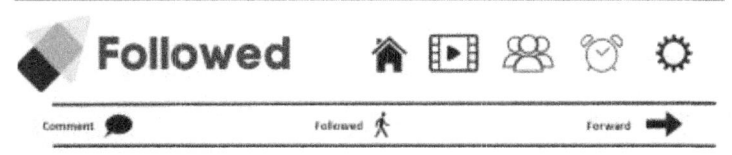

**Followed**

Comment  Followed  Forward

**Ashley McLellan**

This is my angel. Yes I'm on two hours of sleep and yes I just looked in the mirror and saw baby spit-up on my blouse and yes my child is probably terrorizing my parents, crawling near the stairs and opening all the cupboards. But look at her smile. #worthit #grateful #ittakesavillage

**Comments:**

> **Reese Graven**
> You are raising such a precious little soul!

> **Luellen Corning**
> OMG look at those dimples!

**Katy Greene**

@this-precious-girl-just-felt-love-for-the-first-time
Tabby was abandoned in a sewer, left to die because its owners thought she was ugly. Well she was just adopted by some farmers in Merced. Now she has all the cuddles and warmth she deserves. This article just shows me that GOD LOVES EVERY SINGLE LIVING THING ON EARTH, AND BLESSINGS ARE ALL AROUND US!

**Comments:**

> **Gracy Loeffler**
> Um, she could get my snuggles anytime!
>
> **Bobby Smith**
> I've been looking into adopting rather than going through a breeder for this very reason. I think I'm going to go with it.

MY HABIT OF scrolling began in college, looking at chicks. People would post whole photo albums from a night at a bar, and I'd click the right arrow on my laptop, photo after photo. Now I still did that, but the experience was different. My honeymoon with people's lives was over. All the things people said, all the phony ways people justified another selfie—it tranquilized and enraged me at once, and I had not begun to wean myself. If anything, my appetite for that anger was growing.

Grayson tossed his empty Lunchable in the garbage. Dizzy was lurking nearby. It didn't make me feel particularly comfortable, the way she neared us in a crouch. I tried not to stare or tell her to go be creepy somewhere else for fear of the wrath that would incite. So I just minded her in my periphery.

When she was so close I could trip over her, she darted into the building just as I was about to say something. Something about Grayson was now different in an unplaceable way, like when someone's eyebrows are gone. His pants were down to his ankles. That's what was different. And to be frank, Grayson was rather hung. Walkie-talkies crackled from the sides of the courtyard. It became ten seconds of Grayson standing naked in front of the school, possibly unaware. Administration circled him. He took a step backward, his ankle caught, and he fell backward into a security guard who did not appear flattered to be gravity's choice.

"Pull up your pants," the adults said in hushed emergency.

I went toward the doorway Dizzy had just darted through.

# (15)

"I WAS TOLD about your incident with Dizzy after lunch," Mrs. Melvin said. I was in the principal's office now, her desk light aimed at me. Was this on purpose, to create the feel of an interrogation? I made a hand visor.

"Sorry, I can't see you," I said. "It feels like I'm in a Broadway musical."

"I keep the office dim," Mrs. Melvin said. "It's meditative. But then I get used to it and forget I'm in darkness."

She leaned forward in her leather chair and flipped the office's switch. Now visible were pictures on her desk. There was younger Mrs. Melvin with tighter cheeks and sharper shoulders, standing with a teenage volleyball team. A faded photo of her whitewater rafting.

"I wanted to get on the same page with you about what happened," she said. "Have you worked with a student like Dizzy before?"

"What do you mean?" I asked to buy myself time, and put it on her, when of course the answer was no.

"At-risk, emotionally disturbed, and-or living with trauma."

"Oh. No."

"For these students, continuity is everything, Cole. This year we've had five teachers stop showing up to work. We're in our first month of school. Our attrition rate is 25 percent for all teachers. But our special ed department is suffering worse. Attrition there is 45 percent. That means each year, our students are having to get to know new teachers, new routines, new personalities. For students with traumas and special needs—which is the makeup of 10-B—that's really difficult. We need teachers our students know not for six months, but four years. If I'm being blunt, it's a lousy situation right now in San Francisco public schools."

"I have a sense of where this is going," I said.

"In your words, please describe what happened between you and Dizzy earlier." Her tone managed to be both serene and perturbed.

"It started with Grayson," I said. "Dizzy rode him all day. On his birthday, no less. Then the lunch situation happened. After that, Dizzy came back to class and called Grayson retarded some more. So yeah, I called her a bitch."

I noticed my shaky breathing, had to clench to prevent my teeth from chattering like skinny kids fresh out of a cold pool.

"She swung at me. I caught it in the air. Which seems to be a pattern since starting this job. And I—I don't really remember what happened after that. I guess now would be as good a time as ever to tell you, I dropped out of college a few years ago. All of this is new to me. I don't mean that as an excuse, but I'm just saying that I'm assuming after this meeting I will need to find a new job. And that I understand."

"And I guess this is as good a time as ever to tell you," Mrs. Melvin said. "Dizzy was found in a car in the parking garage at Sutter and Stockton. She's currently in foster care on Treasure Island. She's had saltine and Tootsie Pop dinners, gone nights without a roof. Have you ever slept outside not by choice, Cole?"

"No."

"Neither have I. These kids deserve much better from the adults in their lives."

"Ma'am, I fully understand that I'm being fired."

"How long have you been working as a paraprofessional?"

"Fifteen days. Ish."

She sighed a sigh that seemed about more than me and this particular dilemma.

"Cole, when I learned about this situation today, I thought, 'Well, that's no good. We don't want our students verbally attacked. We need good examples in their lives.' But then I considered what hasn't worked out in Dizzy's life: suspensions, ankle monitors, the carousel of weak, absent adults. What she does not need right now is another person who runs away because his feelings got hurt. That's what she does, pushes people away, tests them. She trusts no one because why should she? She's in need of someone who will be there. After what Dizzy did to poor Grayson today, we're probably looking at a suspension for her."

Mrs. Melvin groaned and took her glasses off and pinched her forehead until it looked like a brain.

"I hate it. It doesn't teach lessons; it grooms them for a life of surveillance, pat downs, parole. It ends up feeling like destiny. Female foster children have something like a 35 percent chance of getting arrested when they turn nineteen."

A burst of static caused Mrs. Melvin to reach for her walkie-talkie and kill it.

"The boys end up being the focus because they are the bulk of the noise, the violence, the danger to each other and society. Their actions stand out more. So the girls in these situations get lost in the shuffle. Left to survive by their own means. It's the great American tragedy. Well, with Dizzy, I fear we're near the end of the road. I've been principal at Seaside for ten years and only expelled three students. Two brought automatic guns. If we lose Dizzy, that means more adults failed her. I won't have it."

I sat quietly, honoring Mrs. Melvin's speech with the space it deserved. How someone could organically compose their thoughts like she just had, I had no idea. It further convinced me that I would never feel like an actual adult in the world.

"She deserves better," I parroted. I hoped that would speed up this termination.

"What would you think about filling in full time with Dizzy through the end of the year?"

My mind was so sure it had just heard, "I wish you the best of luck finding a suitable career," that my lips were shaped to say, "Thank you," and I set my feet to stand and walk out of the room. I stopped myself.

"I'm sorry?" I asked.

"Would you be interested in being Dizzy's one-on-one, full time, to help see that she graduates at the end of the year?"

My instinct was no. But I had a vision suddenly: me sitting on our couch, late morning, the long antidepressant infomercials on ESPN describing me—"Can hardly convince yourself to move? Don't want to see anyone? Don't think your life has value?" Swiping through Followed posts of people's 5k runs and cats. Jacking off, feeling immediately sadder. Falling asleep to SportsCenter, waking up to Isaac getting home, sitting up to try to look like I hadn't been lying there all afternoon. This vision suffocated me, let no light through.

"You're a city kid, aren't you?" Mrs. Melvin asked.

"Yes."

"I thought so. Something about the way you sit. Or talk. Or your eye contact. Which school?"

"Merced High."

"I guess that's the city."

"Where did you go?" I asked, defensive.

"Saint Ignatius."

"Psh." This being the natural response to learning anyone went to SI.

"The point is, kids can smell it on someone, whether they're from here," Mrs. Melvin said. "A lot of people come in from Seattle or DC with their Teach For America certificate and Gandhi fantasies and get chewed up by these kids in less than a year. It's gotten as predictable as my soap operas. We need people from the city helping these kids, even if they're from Merced or SI. That will have to do because most people who were born and raised here—the ones who could truly make a difference for these kids—they're long gone, moved away or worse. So what do you say?"

She saw my daze.

"Just sit on it for a night," she said. "If you're in my office tomorrow at eight to fill out some paperwork, I'll know I've got a new hire. If you're not, I'll know I don't."

"All right."

She looked at me weird. "What movie?" she asked.

"Huh?"

"The quote. What movie?"

I closed my eyes, then unflexed my face. "I actually don't

know what you just said."

"*Godfather*? Part two? Come on... Geez. How can I trust a man who can't mindlessly throw around *Godfather* quotes?" Mrs. Melvin asked. "Perhaps, 'I've made an offer you can't refuse'?"

I nodded, as in "Good one." Then the static of the walkie-talkie returned, and I left. As I walked toward the bus stop, I saw a RAV4 with its caution lights on. Grayson was making his way across the street.

"Hey, Grayson!" I called. "Happy birthday!"

Grayson stopped in the middle of the road. His truncated arm waved. "Thanks! You too!"

## OCTOBER 2010: IN A HEARTBEAT

# ISAAC

## (16)

AT GO©, I was put on Operation Land Lens, an initiative that, prior to my hire, had web-mapped Mexico, the United States, and Canada. And with this new wave of hires, they were looking at taking on the rest of the physical world. Investment money was poured into satellite systems. GO© purchased information when necessary, though from whom was a little more hushed. And finally, the most critical information to creating an accurate digital mapping system came from actual humans in little cars with rotating gizmos that captured real-time 360-degree panoramas of the surroundings. Cole and I saw them driving around our neighborhoods at all hours, late at night getting off the bus, on foggy mornings toward hangover pho; the cars looked like what would be produced if the Delorean from *Back to the Future* and an insect had sex. Thanks to this, GO© now had data relevant to 75 percent of the world's population. Three thousand cities. Fifty countries. Five million miles of roads. I was joining a machine.

I tried to be at my desk and logged in by 9:30 every morning, where for much of my day I tweaked map flaws. Monarch was the in-house software used for this. It had satellite and street-view technology with an algorithm that deciphered street signs and their meanings. The smoothness of GO© operations also relied on the help of real-life users, who had the power to report problems and submit comments, called "issues." I was surprised by the willingness of regular people to participate. They weren't getting paid, had no vested interest in the growth of this company. It must have given them a sense of purpose to alert us: "Maps told me to take a left here, but the sign says no left turn," or, "This is no longer a bookstore, it is now Greens n Things."

Issues like this were steadily sent to me, adding to my queue. For the first couple weeks, it gave me anxiety, how the list never shrank. But I got the hang of Monarch. Just a click and a drag made a change official. I could draw new roads, edit the curvature of existing ones, draw polygons that represented parks or bodies of water. It was like real-life Sims, life imitating art. The coolest thing was, green dots all over the cartoon maps represented an uncensored, panoramic view of that location. In my first month, I saw a kid flipping off the camera in Cape Town, a woman sunbathing naked in Perth.

Of course, I had some reservations over my role with the company, the idea of every inch of the world being mapped, thus, in a way surveilled. Surely a consequence of this project was not just a loss of the hidden gems of our world, the delicacies of the unknown, but also privacy. I'd seen enough doomsday movies to know how this could shake out. Robots frying us, people ratting on family and neighbors to save themselves.

I also hesitated to be all-aboard on the GO© culture and resisted diving headfirst into any hype. Some dudes were lost in the GO© sauce, probably slept in their company embroidered vests. I'd listened as they managed to reroute discussions back to whatever project they were working on at the moment. A ping-pong of unremarkable stories, like machines whose genius took up all the space. My whole life up until this point, I never had anything going on; I didn't understand why these people wanted to be so obvious about it.

But then again, hearing the clicking of keyboards, the air thick with brainwork, I felt banded in, part of something profound. Maybe it was in my mind, but I could feel my vocabulary expanding. My thoughts came quicker. Less musing, considering a funny scenario, more getting to the point and staying on it. Working at GO© was like being surrounded by a breed of man that accessed more than the 10 percent of brain an average person was limited to, and that feeling was druglike, not that I'd ever done any drugs.

## (17)

I BECAME ACQUAINTANCES with two dudes from upstate New York: Kevin and Ward, who already knew each other from Colgate and moved out West together. The East Coast me and Cole. Ward had an unignorable lisp, which he seemed to overcompensate for by dispatching opinions. His parents were divorced, his dad some big-shot banker, his mom a Botox goddess, in Ward's words. I could tell he resented them but had an allergy to processing his emotions and preferred his childhood to remain a piece of gravel in his oxfords. Kevin, taller and quieter, rowed at Colgate and still rowed in the mornings in the port of Redwood City before work. He wore glasses with circular rims and always came to work with shirt shoulders wet. He was one of those guys who you knew what he'd look like at fifty. Bald, unblemished, featureless. Ward and Kevin had a shared religion of Springsteen and the Mets. I think my knowledge of contemporary music and sports—and some primitive likeness in shape and posture—matched us as friends on our floor.

We hung out for the first time one afternoon when GO© sent out a companywide email that Tom Morello was coming by for an impromptu concert on the lawn. I planned to go, stand in the back, and see if he converted any Rage songs to acoustic. Just as I was about to log off for the day, a chat window from GO©'s internal messaging system appeared on my screen. It was from Ward:

> Me and K are heading out to catch TM in a min. In?

The dopamine of this message wasn't the level of a secret admirer note, but it wasn't far off. I replied:

> Def

I deliberated for a moment, stared at the screen. I typed thank you, considered what it would look like, then sent it.

I met them at the Blue Moon spigot in the GO©-To Cafe and followed them to the sounds of ambient distortion. Outside it was a perfect 75, aromatic of cut grass. There was probably a crowd of thirty or forty GO© employees standing within reach of Tom Morello. I was so close I could read the Converse logo on his shoe. He still wore the guitar right beneath his chin, almost like a violin. He stomped his feet like he was playing high-octane metal again.

Ward leaned in and whispered. "Favorite Rage album. Go."

Kevin put his index finger to his chin. "Probably *Battle of LA*."

"Such a newb answer," Ward said.

"I gotta go *Evil Empire*," I said. "That was my life in middle school. I could probably still recite 'Bulls On Parade.'"

"Fair," Ward said. "I think I gotta go with self-titled. So iconic. Brought so much to center stage, musically by merging heavy metal and rap, socially by bringing political activism into music."

Morello performed what sounded like explorational feedback, some arpeggiated riffs, and of course his trademark DJ-scratching sounds. When songs finished, GO© employees politely flashed the devil horn sign. Tom Morello smiled, pressed his hands together in thanks. I remembered an old VHS video of a Rage concert, slow-mo footage of seas of people jumping to government-lambasting choruses. I wondered how it felt to do a corporate gig after what he'd stood for his whole career.

Morello's guitar had a sticker that said, "ARM THE HOMELESS."

"That sticker is sick," Ward said.

"So sick," someone said somewhere.

When the gig was over, it felt odd for there not to be a booming chant from tens of thousands of people for an encore. Morello didn't say much beyond some gentle words into the mic that I didn't catch, then a guy went up and asked him to autograph his laptop case.

"Me and Kev are about to go grab beers at El Toronado," Ward said. "Care to join?"

We caught the evening GO© bus, which crawled through Friday rush hour on the 101 all the way to Haight Street, where we got off and entered a land of beers I didn't know existed. Rows of taps, a kaleidoscope of pint glass shapes. When it was my turn, I ordered a beer based on its witty name and got served black tar in a wine glass. Ward eyed me.

"This is actually good," I said. When I finished, I felt concussed.

We walked across the street to a bar with TVs to catch some postseason baseball. The Giants were in the embryonic stages of a miracle. They'd been so putrid in recent years, people resisted the idea that they had a chance. But that didn't mean the bars weren't packed, everyone wearing their Tim Lincecum shirts with his crooked face and stoner charm. Having grown up in Riverside, I couldn't claim to be a Giants fan, but it was exciting to be in a big-market sports city with one of its teams in the playoffs.

Innings went by, and I realized I hadn't said anything in a while. Ward and Kevin were conversing naturally in the way of old friends. I caught words like "liquid" and "short term." I got worried that I didn't have what it took to sustain an interesting friendship with successful people. All my life I'd spent around ballplayers, and though I never behaved like them or felt like one of them, I never felt insecure around them either. Rather, I'd grown into my role as other with them. I needed something to say, something to add. On the TV, Lincecum did what looked like a gymnastics floor routine, and out came a mid-nineties fastball.

"It was at University of Washington," I said. "Lincecum hit 97 in that game."

I wasn't sure how I had introduced this story. Typical of 9 percent beer, I was speaking first and realizing it after. But their faces told me their prior conversation was less appealing than what they'd just heard.

"This was three years ago. I remember sitting by the space heater in the dugout," I continued, "watching all the scouts in their peacoats squint at their radar guns in disbelief. Cole came up to the heater in between innings and put his hands up to it. Together we watched Lincecum throw darts. Cole of course had heard about Timmy. We all had. The snaggly phenom of the Pac-10. It excited Cole, the challenge of pitching against him."

At that point, he was a year away from the wild pitches, the boos from the crowd, sleeping on my floor curled under a blanket after his games, watching bad movies to pacify him to sleep.

"The snow really started coming down in the middle of the fourth. Cole came back to the dugout after buzz-sawing through their lineup—three up, three down—took his hat off, shook out the ice, slid on a beanie, blew double snot rockets. I said something like, 'Touching.' And he was like, 'Yeah, well, you wouldn't understand.'"

Ward smiled.

"Were you a benchwarmer or something?"

"Lifetime achievement in that category," I said

Ward and Kevin looked at each other and laughed, almost impressed, as if self-deprecation was a level in a video game they had not yet reached.

"There was a running joke that our coach didn't even know who I was," I said. "Cole said on the plane to Washington that I was only on the traveling roster was so the team could eat me if we crashed in the wilderness."

Ward leaned over the counter and mimed another round.

"Did it ever bother you?" Kevin asked. "As a competitor, as a friend, him talking to you like that?"

"Not if you knew him. In the middle of that game, when he should have been putting all his focus into his pitching, he said, 'Someday we'll get you an AB, Isaac Moss.'"

"Wait, sorry to interrupt, I'm locked into this story. But you'd never had a single at-bat?" Ward asked.

"At that point? No."

"How long had you been there?"

"Three years."

"Jesus Christ!"

"Cole won that game," I said. I looked up at the TV. "Beat Lincecum in his house. And for the rest of the series, Cole dedicated himself to sending Coach subliminal hints to give me my first at-bat. He'd go up to just within an earshot of Coach, hide inside a doorway or behind a pillar, and whisper my full name all seductive—Issssaac Mosssssss...Issssaac Mossssss—making Coach spin around, spooked. And Cole would just look forward, straight faced. I don't know how."

"So?" Ward asked. "Did it work?"

"In the series finale, Coach actually told me to grab a bat and get in the on-deck circle. I took off my beanie and snow gloves, took practice hacks with the donut, feeling more like an imposter than an actual ballplayer. There were two outs, so I was expecting to go back to the dugout. But the snow was brutal, and a slippery ball hit the batter and kept the inning alive. My name got announced on the loudspeaker for the first time in college. It felt like a dream—not a dream come true, but more like something impossible."

"What happened?" Kevin asked, antsy.

"I worked a full count and flew out to the pitcher."

"Oh no!" Kevin yelled.

"And as I was jogging back into the dugout, Cole was outside the dugout, clapping his snow gloves, calling bravo!"

"I gotta meet this guy ASAP," Kevin said.

"Yeah, Isaac, make it happen," Ward said. It was the tone of someone used to being accommodated, but I couldn't deny that to be the subject of demand felt like belonging.

I didn't tell them what Cole's gesture meant to me. The reality was, I never really wanted the at-bat. I was already resigned to who I was in college baseball. A team historian type. But that didn't change the fact that the at-bat never would've happened without Cole, and I didn't have any other friends who would've thought to do that or, really, other friends at all.

"U-Dub retired Lincecum's number after that season," I said. "He got drafted by the Giants tenth overall. Now we're watching him on TV. Cole...he was out of baseball a year later."

Kevin and Ward were bewitched.

"Another story, another time," I said mythically.

"My curiosity is tumescent," Ward said.

"So what's he up to now?" Kevin asked. "At least give us that."

I checked my watch. I'd bought one, having noticed that everyone at work wore one. There was a balance, I was finding, to being independent, which GO© encouraged with slogans like "bring your authentic self," but not too independent, to the point of ignoring the unspoken norms of the upper middle class. A watch seemed like the right call, plus I had to admit, it felt tastefully adult to shoot my wrist out and look at it.

It was 10:45.

"Right now? I'd say Cole's probably at home, watching *Cops* reruns."

# COLE

## (18)

DIZZY WAS SUSPENDED for three days for pantsing Grayson. Without Dizzy's schedule to follow, I observed the other students in the class. They left certain periods—Delfino to gym, O'Shea to art, Grayson to history—then eventually returned to their home base, 10-B. Some afternoons Mr. Antonini did word problems involving millimeters; other times he broke out some Spanish, which felt spontaneous. Mostly I sat with Grayson, who read picture books until he got distracted and asked my opinions on a facet of Batman. Delfino and O'Shea bickered one minute, then fraternized the next over music videos with twerking models or Google images of shoes. When the classroom was empty, Mr. Antonini filled me in on the students' backgrounds.

O'Shea lived with his dad and grandma in the Tenderloin, took the 49 to school every morning. His dad was thirty-four years old, had O'Shea when he was eighteen and a basketball megastar at Balboa High. He worked as a janitor at Warriors games now, took O'Shea often. One night Monta Ellis gave O'Shea his game shoes. O'Shea sold them on eBay. In class he was always scrolling images of haircuts and admiring his own in his phone camera, the swooping images buzzed on the sides of his head. He ran a small operation in the boys locker room, $5 a haircut, which the football and basketball team constantly took him up on. He had a short fuse for corniness or adults in any capacity, with their tired methods of steering him on the right path. He had talent and curiosity for the world unless it was forced on him, at which point you lost him.

"How you got yo arm muscles?" O'Shea asked me on my second day. "You be eatin' at Outback?"

Delfino didn't ask many questions. He didn't take to the gentle encouragement of Mr. Antonini either. Despite his proclivity for fights, he sucked his thumb. Mr. Antonini told me about Delfino's childhood in cars, his dad pimping his mom out in alleys, until both parents were out of the picture. That Delfino was showing up to school was a win. Anything else was a bonus, given what he'd lived.

Majique was Dizzy's friend, the one with her in the corner store on my first day. She was new to Seaside, arriving at the beginning of the academic year from Modesto with no file. Mr. Antonini knew nothing other than she moved in with her grandma in Fillmore and gravitated toward Dizzy as the only other girl in the class, guarded her around grabby boys. With Dizzy suspended, I'd seen Majique in the hallways, in the courtyard, but not in class.

When Dizzy returned and I was still there, she halted. All morning she refused to let me sit by her. I'd be across the room minding my own business, and all of a sudden she'd go, "Don't look at me, plumber."

In the hall I traveled five or six steps behind her, the closest she'd allow. I felt like Secret Service to the president's daughter on a trip to the mall. She walked slowly, stopped at classroom doors, knocked on them, then walked away. Eventually Dizzy and Majique reached room 445, where Mr. Salsbury taught history. Mr. Antonini sent some of his students here to integrate with standard classes. It was called mainstreaming. I'm not sure why, but the word made me think of old books about religions that forced people to believe certain things or die. Mr. Salsbury came into the hall making urgent motions with his hand. In pleated slacks, a San Francisco zoo shirt, and sandals, he looked like the quirky survivor of an apocalypse years later. "Allstar" by Smash Mouth could be heard from inside his room.

"Class is starting, ladies," he said.

The girls walked around him.

"OK, so. Let's everyone grab a seat," he said, turning down the warm-up jams. I sat far away from Dizzy near students I'd never met.

"We got a Do Now on the board," Mr. Salsbury said.

"I seen Clara roll her eyes at me across the courtyard," Dizzy said to Majique.

"Remember when her mama come to school to punk Allegra for breakin' her Nextel?" Majique asked.

Dizzy shrieked with laughter, commanding the class's attention. Mr. Salsbury understood this moment would not be stifled and so let it breathe temporarily.

"Clara be on her Nextel like *beep* *Mama school done come pick me up. Over.*"

Majique slapped the table in laughter. "I can't breathe, bitch," she said.

"Girls. We're five minutes into class now," Mr. Salsbury said gently.

"Bitch think 'cause she beefy nobody gonna step to her," Dizzy said. "I'll bust her fat-ass watermelon head."

Majique clapped.

"Oh God, she hella jiggly. You seen her doing layups in PE?"

Their laughter reached new levels.

"So, guys?" Mr. Salsbury said. "Yesterday, we...so, phones away, guys. Please. Or points off for your tribes."

I began to feel guilty sitting there as this man floundered. Technically I was a teacher too, sort of. At least an adult. I could have tried to assist him to bring his class together.

"Dizzy. OK. You can earn a point for your tribe by answering this question," Mr. Salsbury said. "What was the result of Colonialists coming to take the land of the Native Americans?"

"Why you pick me? It's hella other students here."

"I care about your education. It's my job."

"You fired."

"Dizzy."

"Iono. They fought?"

"Actually, that's correct."

Dizzy stood on the desk and presented herself pageant-like.

"Aye, lemme get at that," said a boy from Equality Tribe.

"Yo eyebrows got warts on it, if you wasn't aware," Majique answered for Dizzy. "So that's a no."

"Majique, please don't get involved," Mr. Salsbury said.

"Oh, I get involved."

The boy from Equality Tribe drew in a breath, chin raised, seeming to scheme his next words.

"Can we reroute this?" Mr. Salsbury asked.

This man's shipwrecked hair—a comb over in both directions, making it go in no direction—reminded me of that guy Trump's hair. That morning on Followed, someone had shared an article from *The Guardian* titled "Fabulous *World of Golf* Host Donald Trump Considers Running for President." In it, Trump said, "I'd love not to, but someone has to do something. We're losing this country." Which I didn't understand. Losing the country how? Was it about Obamacare? Everyone seemed to be pissed about that. I didn't know Trump, but he didn't strike me as someone concerned about his health or anyone else's. I was as aggressively uninformed as it came, but I doubted anyone could change anything in four years anyway. Especially someone with that hair. And Mr. Salsbury's hair looked inspired by or in competition with it.

"Dang, I'm feeling bad for Integrity Tribe right now, Dizzy," he said. "You just lost them a point." He went to the board and erased a tally as Dizzy continued to dance on the tabletop.

"Mr. Salsbury a gay-ass worm," a voice whispered somewhere.

Dizzy sat back down. My attention was drawn to a noise in the ceiling, where a rectangle piece was loose. It fell out and came flitting down, landing on Dizzy's head. She swatted and scooted her chair back. Where the piece of ceiling had been was now black, like a missing tooth.

"It's rats up there?" Dizzy asked.

Mr. Salsbury held up his hands like a maestro, as though this enigma might bring the class to order at last.

"I do not fuck with rats!" Dizzy yelled.

"Bitch, you from the island. Rats being all in your domicile is a fact," a boy said.

"Fuck you, Ivan, in yo Tempur-Pedic shoes."

Ivan made an unsettling noise with his mouth. I stared blankly at the hole in the ceiling as Dizzy and Ivan beefed. Dizzy slapped Ivan's buzz cut scalp, and he shoved her by the collarbone. She threw such a fast fist I didn't see where it landed on Ivan. One day back from suspension. One strike away from expulsion, throwing blows. She'd be gone soon, I thought, if not for this, something else. It was inevitable, and I knew it was cutthroat to think it was deserved, but after a while, how many bozo decisions can a person make? Ivan ran out of the classroom, likely a precaution to avoid a consequence for shoving a girl. And Dizzy sat in her seat, breathless, looking at the hole in the ceiling.

"So the indigenous tribes," Mr. Salsbury said, as if what just happened was chill. "They were all like, 'Yo, we're peaceful, come to our communities, eat our corn so you can be—'"

"How the roof about to just fall like that?" Dizzy asked.

"Dizzy."

It just came out of my mouth. I didn't know why, but this was the moment I chose to insert myself.

"Nobody talking to you. You irrelevant," Dizzy said.

Her foot bounced. Mr. Salsbury said nothing. There was an escalating energy in the silence. Students respected it, like locals in a tsunami zone and I was the tourist still sunbathing as the water receded.

"And so are you," I said.

"I know you not talking to me."

"This man is here to help," Mr. Salsbury said, clearly not knowing my name.

"False," Majique ruled.

"It's a roof," Dizzy said with less intensity, her focus on something deeper than our squabble. "How the roof about to be made outta cardboard?"

"Well, Dizzy," Mr. Salisbury said, "that's actually a good question. A lot of jewelry is like that. Lots of quote-unquote *silver* is just zinc. Lots of diamonds are cubic zirconia. Much of the world is something presenting itself as something much better. If you don't have the money, like public schools, you get the imitation."

"But ain't the roof supposed to be sturdy? 'Cause it got us under it?"

"A lot of roofs are made of that material. Imagine if that had been made of plaster or marble, and it fell on your head."

"You got a wife?" Dizzy asked.

"That is not a discussion for class," said Mr. Salsbury.

"Translation: no," Majique said.

"When you wife a girl up, how you gonna know you ain't gettin' her Cuban sharkonia?"

"They have ways of telling."

"Watch his ass get punked by a jeweler," Majique said.

"Pff," Dizzy laughed and clicked her lead pencil, which seemed to bring the chaos to a close. Mr. Salisbury had a window in which he was able to teach. Before passing period, Majique heated Cup Noodles in Mr. Salsbury's microwave.

Dizzy and Majique walked across the courtyard toward 10-B, and I trailed. It brought me back to high school, the smell of cheap food and the ocean, the ancient ketchup packets fused to the ground.

"On everything I'ma bank Clara's shit though," Dizzy said,

then punched her fist into her palm. "Chicken bucket bitch."

"Her clothes is like wet dog," Majique said. They fell into whisper.

I leaned in, trying not to be obvious. I wondered about the roots of this conflict. Was it years in the making? Or arbitrary as an annoying face?

Majique forked a tangle of noodles, lifted them so they hung like a wig. Dizzy cupped her hands, communion-like. Majique lowered the noodles into her friend's hands. Dizzy blew on her palms, then slurped. She wiped her palms on her jeans, then held her hands out for more.

"You can go," Dizzy snapped at me, and I fell back to my permitted distance.

# ISAAC

## (19)

THERE WAS AN EOQ3 meeting for the OLL team, led by Audrey, in which she went over some highlights from the quarter. We learned that a GO© streetview cam in Panama City, Florida, had located a missing child who was returned safely to her family. Issue claim #AB71207—a road glitch corrected by yours truly, Isaac Moss, Badge #0237—led a family's survival in freezing temperatures in Norden, California. In the small bright room, I received a golf applause.

"Woot woot!" Audrey said and smiled at me. Over tikka masala, Audrey pep-talked us more about the strides of GO©, what was on the horizon for OLL with regard to projects and team-building events. At the end of lunch, we all got gift cards to REI with the note: "You're meant to traverse."

"Pretty sick stuff, lad," Kevin said after and patted my back.

"Yeah, well done. You gotta think that's what they remember when deciding who to hire full time," Ward said.

Later in the day, Audrey sent out a companywide email.

---

Subject: THIS AFTERNOON, BE THERE OR BE AN EQUILATERAL RECTANGLE

Message: Birthday party in the Organic Garden B at 4:00. You bring your festive vibes. I'll bring Cake ☺

---

This set the office abuzz. I was hearing laptops clap shut left and right. I didn't want to be obviously not working, so I sat at my computer and screwed around on YouTube, pulled up Lonely Planet videos, "I'm On A Boat," and "Like a Boss." My group chat with Ward and Kevin popped up. Ward wrote:

> I think we earned an early Friday boys

Kevin replied:

> Giggity

I went into the bathroom to style my hair. I had no idea what I was doing and walked out looking the same. The three of us met outside, where there was already chatter. From somewhere, I heard someone say "Prolonging the Magic" and "Sacramento." A band was setting up, and with the words I'd just heard at the front of my consciousness, I made the connection that on stage was John McCrea, lead singer of Cake, adjusting his mic in a straw hat. Then there was Vince DiFiore in his backwards beret playing warm-up scales into a hedge. How many times in high school had I watched the "Going the Distance" music video, ironically about a dude ditching his corporate job? The crowd's excitement was growing; nearly any moderate '90s music listener dug Cake. *Fashion Nugget* wasn't quite a frontrunner, but was definitely in the running for my Deserted Island Album, "Italian Leather Sofa" and "Sad Songs and Waltzes" being very underrated songs, in my opinion.

"Holy shit. Audrey! That wizardess! She brought Cake the *band*!" Ward said. He did some calf raises in excitement. "I love Cake!"

Audrey was talking to GO©'s chief culture officer, holding a 5-Hour Energy. I watched her sip the small vial like Alice in Wonderland. A guitar chord filled the walled-in space. A corner keg was flowing with a tasty pumpkin ale from Dogfish Head. John McCrea nodded at Audrey that they were ready, and she skipped up to him and he handed her the mic.

"Before we kick this party off, we're gonna do a little trivia because we all know deep down we're all nerds!" Audrey said.

We all clapped.

"We've got some pretty rad shwag to give away as prizes."

Those who knew Cake slowly moved toward the stage; those who were clearly not '90's white people receded to the edge of the crowd.

"All right. Question one. True Cake connoisseurs may recognize this playful noise, often found in the band's now distinctive sound. Listen," Audrey said. She reached up to McCrea, who passed down what looked like a mousetrap. Audrey palmed it, and it rattlesnaked across the courtyard.

"What is this instrument called?"

"Oh!" Ward raised his hand. "Is it a, like, vibraslap?"

He clearly knew this was the answer but wanted it to sound like a stab in the dark. "Ding ding ding!" Audrey said, then hit the instrument again and everyone laughed.

John McCrea honored Ward with a raised eyebrow. Audrey produced a slingshot, took a balled-up shirt, and shot it at him.

"Thank you, middle school band!" Ward said loudly and shrugged.

"OK! One more question, different shirt," Audrey said. "People have enjoyed Cake for a long time. I've been listening to you guys," she turned to them, "since high school. No, I am not telling any of you how old I am! But they've been around and have even found themselves in some of our favorite movies. In particular, Cake was featured on the soundtrack of this funny movie last year."

"Oh shit!"

Ward stretched his arm as high as it would go.

"Quite the Cake scribe, aren't you, Ward?" Audrey said.

"That would be *Forgetting Sarah Marshall*."

He took a few steps forward to be sure the slingshot could reach him with his second Cake shirt.

"Ah, Ward," Audrey said. "*Forgetting Sarah Marshall* was '08!" I thought I detected pleasure in her tone, perhaps for the added suspense. I found it sexy.

"*I Love You, Man!*" I blurted. People looked at me uneasy. "The movie."

I had to get it out quick before Ward rebounded with the right answer. I didn't know him well yet, but I got the feeling he derived self-worth out of these little battles of the mind.

"Is that...Isaac?" Audrey asked, shielding her eyes until they locked on mine. "Isaac with the epic snag!"

She put the shirt in the slingshot and pulled it far back. I could see her peering mischievously at me between the V. She released the shirt, and I caught it inches from my face. My GO© colleagues oohed, as though my hand-eye coordination was evidence of some higher intelligence. Audrey lowered her weapon to her waist but held my eyes. I unrolled my shirt, and it was a print of the cover to *Prolonging the Magic*. I couldn't remember the eyes of a crowd on me like this for any reason, even in my years of baseball. As minor a moment as this was, I couldn't help but think of Cole, who had a similar feeling night after night as the subject of fanfare and worship from thousands. I could understand the addiction and the disorientation of it vanishing one day, never to return.

Audrey and I stood beside each other for most of the concert, though we didn't talk. Our heads nodded when songs we knew began. At times, our eyes met while singing the same thing. She did a convincing job of quickly turning her head away and raising her hands up to show this was general fun, that there was no spark between us.

Cake played "Wheels," the song from *I Love You, Man*. John McCrea held his hands out in a "behold," gesture at the gray walls of GO©'s compound: "Wheels keep on spinning round, spinning round, spinning round."

Audrey cheered. She wasn't above a good-humored jab. I asked if she wanted the wheels to spin us into another pumpkin ale. She twisted her nose cutely, then put up her hands in surrender. I told her I'd get it, and as I passed her, I felt the elbow of her coat brush mine.

# COLE

## (20)

IN THE HALLS I was seeing fliers for a Seaside High drama production, a play on teen angst, "With opening remarks from Mayor Gavin Newsom!" Pictured on the flier was the cast, their arms folded like they were posing for a grunge album cover. Mayor Newsom stood beside them in the photo, showing his age in subtle ways, gray strands wisping above his sideburns. Still dapper and poised as ever. Passing the fliers made me want to reach into the photo and pull myself in, back to our lunch at Tommy's Joynt. It made me wonder so much. What if I'd chosen USF over Fresno? Had the baseball gods punished me for leaving my city? Would I still have wound up with no college degree, making an unlivable wage in my hometown had I chosen a different path?

On the day of the play, Mr. Antonini suggested Dizzy attend. Everyone in 10-B needed a breather.

"The mayor of San Francisco will be there, Dizzy," he said.

"He hella phony."

"Go learn about teen angst. You're not alone."

"No."

"Dizzy, this is a get-out-of-class pass. Since when is that not at the peak of your pyramid of needs?"

"Shut up."

"Please."

The line for the assembly was chaos. Teachers with eroding posture were swallowed one by one by the auditorium archways. A teacher who couldn't have been any younger than

60 had green hair and a purple sweater, a sort of fatigued Joker. Her students were a human knot unraveling. I anticipated Dizzy would wander off once inside. I wouldn't try to command her. I refused to play that little game like every other adult at the school, who showed her patience and nurturing only to get dookied on in return.

Inside the dark auditorium, the lights of students' phones floated like angler fish. A petite silhouette directed students to fill up all the seats: "No saving seats. No skipping rows."

"You two, here," she said.

"Us?" I asked.

"There."

"You got me fucked up," Dizzy said. "Tellin' me to sit wit the plumber."

"You want to see the production?" she shot. "It's where you're going to have to sit! It's going to be a packed house. There's news coverage. The mayor is here!"

"This Oompa-Loompa better get out my face," Dizzy said.

"We don't have to talk to each other," I told her softly. "Just...you won't even see me. Come on, can we not turn this into a thing?"

I sat. The old woman herded Dizzy into her seat and disappeared into darkness before Dizzy could behead her.

"I don't know what you hate me so much for anyways," I said. "You pantsed a kid and got called out."

"What you need to do? Is address yo nostril hair. Period."

We proceeded to whisper-curse each other through Newsom's entire introduction, which I realized when the auditorium filled with applause. Newsom walked off the stage, out of my life again. Admittedly, it was better that way, to have not seen him, heard his cadence, and been dragged back to a better time.

The lights on the stage turned on. The curtain slid from the middle, revealing the opening scene: a school counselor sitting across from a student. The counselor's costume was a white smock, looking more like a butcher. In the opening dialog, the student told the counselor she was stressed from homework, plus early swimming practice, plus AP physics tutoring.

"SPEAK UP!" Dizzy shouted.

The counselor asked the student: Have you been taking your medication lately? The student sighed dramatically. Yes, she had, but she didn't like the way antidepressants made her feel. Lately, it felt like she was traveling in a dark tunnel. Her life didn't feel real. The faces she passed in the halls were expressionless, like ghosts, and it felt like her legs were cemented to the ground. She pressed her hands to her head as though checking for a fever.

"THIS GIRL LIT!"

"Geez, Dizzy," I said, but nothing more. What could actually be said to her that wouldn't just blow everything up?

The scene continued. The student confessed to having disturbing thoughts. What kind of thoughts? the counselor asked. You wouldn't understand! Curtains. Dead applause. The curtains reopened to Scene Two: the girl sitting on a couch with her mom and dad. Dad said they were worried about her because she hadn't been herself. They were disappointed in her recent report card. Mom said she would never get into UCLA with those grades. Our family has a long history of UCLA, said the mom. If you get rejected, you will bring the family dishonor. The student said she'd been thinking about community college to give her time to find her passion. The crowd applauded in support. The mom yelled, unacceptable! Dad put his hand on Mom's thigh. The student yelled, I'm depressed! Mom scoffed: depression. Well, maybe we can help, Dad said. What's on your mind, sweetie? Well? She looked up. Mom? Dad? She blinked. I'm a lesbian.

"HA!" Dizzy belted.

I'd rather die than have a lesbian daughter, the mother said.

"DISRESPECTFUL BITCH!"

Dizzy roared this so seamlessly it was as if it was part of the play. Inspired by Dizzy, the audience began to let loose whoas and boos. The wheels were coming off, and I was thankful for the dark to hide my amusement. The protagonist of the play's life got worse: Her friends didn't want to hang out anymore because she was moody. She got kicked off the swim team for smoking cigarettes. The number of times she told someone "just leave me alone!" was incalculable. At some point, as though choreographed, Dizzy and I stood up and walked out. We got it: The girl was stressed. We walked out the school entrance into the biting air of Bay Street.

"Those actors was so canister," she said.

We turned a corner and walked around the block. When she and I reached the school entrance, we continued for another lap. Dizzy kicked an Arizona can. When I caught up to it, I kicked it, and then she kicked it again.

"You from the city?" she asked. "Like really?"

"Yeah."

"Where you grew up?"

"The Sunset."

"You swam in the ocean?"

"Couple times, dumbly. You know how cold that is."

"I never been."

"To the ocean? I thought you live on Treasure Island."

"Yeah," she said. "Can't nobody swim on TI. Ain't no beach. You ain't never been?"

"I guess I haven't."

"What's yo last name?"

"Gallegos."

"You a Mexican?"

"Kind of. Technically."

"No you ain't."

"I know. I don't know what I am. How about you?"

"Ain't it obvious?"

"No."

Dizzy kicked the Arizona can, and it boomeranged ahead.

"I don't know," she said. "Why you took this job? Instead of working downtown wit all the squares that's yo age, eatin' brunch."

"Do I look like I like brunch?" I asked. Somewhere a car honked.

"Nah, you right," she said. "You look like you about to shoot up the post office."

# (21)

HALLOWEEN MORNING WAS weather that tricked you to underdress, sunny but icy. As I entered the courtyard, a gust turned a pile of trash into a tornado. It slid around, then the gust died and it disassembled. I watched a Sarah Palin costume in wire glasses and sweeping bangs walk by. Then Michael Jackson in a Jheri curl wig and tinfoil suit. In the hallway to 10-B, beneath the flickering light, was a girl in blue face paint, a character from *Avatar*, I knew, without having seen the movie yet. Everyone was telling me I had to see it. Which made me want to see it less. Isaac had actually been saving the movie to watch for the first time with me. I hadn't ever seen him anticipate something like this. He'd tried to persuade me many a weeknight. Like, could the film be that fucking good? But still, I knew I should watch it with my friend. If the roles were reversed and I was excited about something and wanted to share it with him, there would be no hesitation from Isaac. I pulled out my phone and texted him:

Halloween movie night tonight? Avatar?

Grayson was waiting outside 10-B in a Giants uniform. White pants, high orange socks. "Good morning, Grayson," I said.

"Notice anything different about me?" he asked.

Mr. Antonini arrived a few minutes late, fumbling to retrieve his keys from his windbreaker. "What up, MVP?" he said.

Grayson and he did their secret handshake, and it made Grayson smile smugly, like they were conspiring to take over the world.

"Most of my students act too cool to dress up for Halloween. Except Grayson. You're not too cool, are you?"

"I'm Cody Ross," he said matter-of-factly.

O'Shea arrived in a *Scream* mask. Before long, he was snoring in his seat. Midway through first period, he jolted awake and fed himself an M&M's fun pack. Watching this put a soreness in me. Not because O'Shea was eating breakfast candy, but because this moment felt like a reminder that I'd metaphorically broken down somewhere on my path to maturity. For instance, take the Sarah Palin costume earlier. Sarah Palin had been in the news a ton lately. I knew the general opinion of her—especially in the Bay Area—was that she was a farce. She'd recently called North Korea an ally. But beyond that, if I was being honest, I knew more about Tina Fey's impersonations of her on *SNL* than the real her.

As an adult, I felt like I owed it to myself, or the world or whatever, to know more. When I scrolled social media, and people shared articles on this topic or others, I wondered if the rest of the world was truly more informed or just toiling to appear that way.

Sitting in 10-B, the insecurity manifested in other ways: Three years of college business classes had taught me everything about production costs and profit. I'd heard "margin" and "yield" a lot. Yet in a different class, I'd been taught that capitalism was wrecking Earth. At which point I dropped out. This left me in a purgatory of knowledge, afraid to have an opinion because the facts in my mind were either contradictory or incomplete, and I was too sad or apathetic to fix that and privileged enough to be unaffected by politics. How it all connected to this morning was, I knew O'Shea's M&M's breakfast was juvenile and dumb, but at the same time, I wished for a bag myself.

"Dizzy on some Godzilla shit down the hall," Delfino warned when he arrived. Mr. Antonini sprang to his feet and locked the door. Moments later it was kicked from the outside.

"Let me in!"

I could hear her breaths, short and erratic.

"On days like this, she's a little extra," Mr. Antonini said. "With the sugar from the candy."

The door was booted again.

"Y'all trying to get me to graduate, but I can't come in for my education."

Mr. Antonini chuckled to himself. "This feels like an actual horror film," he said.

"Mr. Cole," Grayson said. "Mr. Cole."

"Yeah, buddy," I said.

"Are you watching the World Series?"

"I am not."

"Oh."

"Hmm," Mr. Antonini said. "Could've fooled me." He eyed me. "You look like the type to take in a ballgame. Don't take that the wrong way."

"I understand."

"You know the Giants are in it, right?"

I'd been asked innocent baseball questions plenty of times, but somehow hadn't honed a scripted response yet. I always just sort of froze, like right now. Of course I knew the Giants were in the fucking World Series. I knew half the dudes competing in this World Series. I'd beaten Lincecum. I'd struck out Mike Fontenot in a summer game once—and what was Fontenot even doing on the Giants' postseason roster anyway? Still, what good were those stories to tell? They would inevitably lead to one very dark one. All those memories were better left unsaid, buried with time.

"MR. ANTONINI A VIRGIN 'CAUSE HE WEAR CARGO PANTS!"

Dizzy sounded like a voice screaming on speaker phone.

"I see yo shoe under the door," Dizzy said at me. "Fuck you then."

"You've already had like two million Snickers," Mr. Antonini called. "Obviously."

"But O'Shea eating hella candy."

"Well, O'Shea is in here minding his own business, if creepily."

From his chair in his murder mask, O'Shea gave a thumbs-up.

"I can't educate you in your state," Mr. Antonini said.

"You know damn well ain't no educating goin' on right now or ever."

"Thank you."

A long silence suggested that Dizzy had left. But there was a fuzz in my arm, a sixth sense that she was out there looming. I couldn't resist peeling down the beige construction paper over the window that protected student confidentiality of 10-B. On the other side, Dizzy peered at me, breathing out her nose, fogging the window. In her hand was something psychedelic green. She reached her arm back and whipped it. The sound was like a piece of gravel or hail pelting a bus window. Even with the door between us, I flinched, and when I opened my eyes, the window was spiderwebbed. Dizzy stood there, huffing, her image fragmented.

I had wanted her to do that. At first, I thought it was because I'd wanted her to do something stupid and reckless already and get it over with. Make my days easier through her self-elimination, allow me to get paid to sit around and field the litany of Grayson's innocent "what ifs?" But looking through the glass, I realized it wasn't the destruction I was drawn to, but the display, the possibility of hitting a small target with a smaller object. The focused, precise fury. And she'd done it, split double-pane glass with a Jolly Rancher. It was the kind of Roy Hobbs moment that made you stop and think about higher powers. Arms like that, I knew, were precious few.

## (22)

FOLLOWING MY NO-HITTER in '07, I couldn't shake that one pitch. In games, I started to have panic attacks that numbed my fingertips. Pitches started to slip out of my hand more, rolling to the backstop or hitting batters. I started aiming the ball, which turned into long homeruns. Teammates kind of looked the other way when near me in the dugout. I got quieter; what was there to say?

Eventually, people started booing, beginning with one or two loudmouths, the type who viewed athletes solely as entertainers. This turned into more boos. Kids did what the adults did. By the end of March, a full inning, three whole outs, felt like one of those bad dreams where you're trying to talk and can't get out a word. In bed after games, I held a baseball until the sun was up and I could hear the birds and the street cleaner from down the block. Baseball felt like a hangover. In my five starts since that one pitch, I had thrown a combined seventeen innings, walked thirty-nine batters, and my record was 0-2.

San Diego State came to town for a series. It would be the first time I had seen Tony Gwynn since turning him down. The matchup was me vs. Stephen Strasburg, the kid who Gwynn had shopped as the number two of our one-two punch. Strasburg had done what Gwynn said he would, risen to first-round status. The local coverage leading up to the game was a beehive. Isaac and I would be sitting on the couch, eating our stupid college dinners, watching *Wheel of Fortune*, and I'd see a commercial advertising the upcoming game. Don't wait, tickets are selling out fast, it said, and showed slo-mos of my strikeouts.

On the day of the game, my hands were shaking two hours before I even went to the field. I walked over to Isaac's room. Like a trusty dog at the window, he was there, as I knew he'd be. I gave my light two-knuckle knock and entered.

"'Sup, horse," he said from his laptop, his stirrups and baseball pants laid neatly across his bed, an endearingly pointless custom for him.

"'Sup?"

It was a nothing question. Isaac could tell, so he offered no response, just watched me jitter my eyes around. I sat on the floor and gathered my knees to my chest.

"You got some pregame vibes, man?" I asked. "Something to shake it up?"

"In a heartbeat," Isaac said.

"Thanks."

"No that's the song. 'In a Heartbeat.'"

"Oh. What is it?"

"*28 Days Later* soundtrack. Seen it?"

"No."

"Great zombie flick."

"You choose this because my life has become a zombie movie?"

"Listen to the buildup, man. It plays when the odds are against our hero, but he goes on a solo rampage, gouges a dude's eyeballs out. I like to think if I was ever about to be in some kind of war, this is the song I'd want on in the tank."

I downloaded the song to my iPod, like with most of his recs. On the way to the ballpark, I saw the liquor store off to the side, went back and forth in my mind, kept on going for a few blocks. Then I turned around and parked. Inside, the cashier gave me a look that told me he knew who I was, probably took his kids to the games, probably knew from the commercials that I was pitching later.

Whatever. I pointed to the plastic bottle of vodka and paid him.

Dusk in Fresno was pretty—sidewalk chalk across the sky. I sat on a bucket in the bullpen, cracked the white cap, poured vodka into the green Gatorade cup, making a satisfying hollow sound. With one sip, a warmth spread through me that pleasantly blurred the lines of things. Reporters were doing pregames with their cameramen in the front rows. Scouts gathered behind home plate with their radar guns and clipboards.

Before warm-ups, I listened to Isaac's song rec. "In a Heartbeat" had a slow, ominous buildup, the musical embodiment of something malevolent in the shadows. Then the climax thrashed with melodic whines—whatever had been lurking had revealed itself, and it did not disappoint; it was to be feared. It was me. Cole Gallegos. Isaac was right about the song. It made me want war. I drank another sincere pull of vodka. Life felt simple then. Isaac was a good friend. And so was baseball. Volatile, but loyal. I felt at ease enough to sign pregame autographs for kids, something I hadn't done in weeks.

"How 'bout that sky, huh, fellas?" I said, signing the underbills of small hats. The children murmured thanks.

Gwynn came across the field and hugged me so tight my back cracked. We took a picture for the media.

"Let's have us a ballgame," Gwynn said, chomping his gum, and I made sure not to get so close that he might smell my breath.

On the mound, my walkout song "Tell Me When To Go" faded out, leaving the air still. The leadoff batter wagged his bat in the box. My first pitch hit him square in the helmet. The booze had quit on me, nuked by my adrenalin. As the batter jogged to first, I looked at my shortstop and pointed to him, the pitcher's way of showing he wasn't fazed and was ready to get a ground ball and turn two. My shortstop just stared blankly, like "I'll believe it when I see it." I'd lost my teammates, a realization that almost took my legs out from under me.

I forgot to come set, balked the guy to second. Then I threw the next pitch from the windup. The runner waltzed to third, smirked as my infielders shouted at me to step off. But I couldn't really hear, couldn't breathe, or I could breathe but oxygen gave me nothing. The crowd ah'd. When I really thought about their sound, I heard pity, but it was layered with something else, some primitive want to see more fascinating failure. Cellphones were out, recording. Grubb took off his mask and looked out at me. Not angrily. Like me, he appeared to be wondering if this was real, and how. Coach Lonnie yanked me in the first inning.

Exiting, I pulled the brim of my hat down so I wouldn't have to see anyone—not the team, not the fans, not Gwynn. I just looked down at the infield grass and watched it scroll by like a film reel. My teammates gathered in front of the dugout to support me or console me or whatever that fucking custom was. I held my hand out like limp lettuce and met theirs just to not show them up. Then I went through the clubhouse and out the stadium to the parking lot to my Buick and drove off.

I went far out into farm country, where acres of corn were purple from the moon. By midnight my pores were sour from old nerves. I got stuck at a red light that refused to change. Minutes passed in idle. I was struck by the pointlessness of this, of me here, of everything. What kept me following this law in the empty dead night? To my left, I spotted a tree in the front yard of a house, through which stars winked. There was a calmness to the tree. From the way its branches bent, I could tell it was bearing fruit. I put the car in park, and when I climbed out, the light turned green.

"Fuck you," I said, my car running at the intersection.

I bent down to pick up stones. A property's light flashed on, showing a domesticated porch. Plastic picnic chair, child's shovel. I froze until fairly certain it had been a motion sensor and not a farmer with a shotgun. Nonetheless, I went to my car and killed the engine and rotated the lights off. Now the darkness and the insects were a sensory overload. I shook the stones in my hand like dice, looked up at the tree. I leaned my back shoulder down. My arm fell snug into its slot. From Little League all the way up, I'd seen all kinds of pitchers. Some threw mechanically, like their dads had taught them from some manual. Others fileted their backs like ladybug wings, clumsy and painful. But not me. There was poetry, romance to my delivery, the kind of thing someone might make a sculpture out of. I remembered my growth spurts as a teen, how I'd flex my arm into my hands, feel its salmon-like tautness, and have the vague sense that I was special.

The first rock I threw missed the tree entirely and kicked across the road. But the next clipped right where the branch held the fruit. There was a thud, and then rolling beside me was something obsidian and waxy. I tucked it in my jersey, then slashed another. A few properties away, a dog yowled. Soon my greed had amassed me a bounty of whatever this fruit was. My accuracy and precision, with only the moon to guide me. This was a rare arm I had.

"I am a stud," I told myself in the darkness.

At home, my roommates were bathed in flat-screen glow, mushing their video game controllers, Double Gulps half-filled with dip spit beside them. No one brought up the game. We all just kind of nodded at each other. I walked past them to Isaac's room with no idea of what time it was, other than I knew he was still up. He was watching *You've Got Mail*. I dragged my blanket to his room and curled myself on the floor.

"Someday you'll lose your virginity," I sighed.

Isaac's silence meant he was taking the high road.

"Where'd you go?" he asked.

"A drive."

"Where?"

"An avocado tree." I rolled over. "Can you put something

else on?"

"Like what?" he asked.

"*Lord of the Rings*. Or some other alternate reality."

Isaac fanned off his covers and went to the DVD shelf, alphabetized.

"It feels like I've been having a heart attack for two months," I said.

"We got Army coming to town," Isaac said. "They've lost like every game this year. Their best hitter is hitting .250 with zero dings. I checked when I got home."

"Oh, yeah."

"They'll be your slump-buster, put you back on top again."

Blogs were predicting my drop in the draft. Somewhere, dudes were getting paid minimal money to pick apart my future, use my psychological breakdown as an opportunity to advance their little journalism lives. I went back and forth about the stakes of this time in my life. Part of me was in this demented zen—perhaps a survival mechanism—able to convince myself there was no rush to recovering from these yips. It would happen when it was ready, and in the meantime, just don't take it too seriously. Then the other side of me would kick in, the one with a paralyzing fear of standing on the mound in front of people, of holding a baseball. The one who knew he had a million-dollar arm but wanted nothing to do with it. The one praying for meteorologically impossible Fresno rain.

# ISAAC

**(23)**

KEVIN AND WARD were fascinated by Cole's story. They Googled his highlights and footage of his yips. Now they wanted to meet him, watch a ballgame with him, which to me was an odd wish. Wasn't it intuitive to assume Cole hated baseball now, that he had some level of PTSD associated with the game? Did this not occur to them? It was this self-interest and disconnect from other people's emotions that I assumed was at the root of divorces and Mazda Miata convertibles at age fifty.

Still, I didn't want to disappoint Kevin and Ward, and I felt Cole would elevate my status among them. That morning I was about to invite Cole out for Halloween plus the World Series Game 4 viewing when I saw he had already texted me:

> Halloween movie night tonight?

Was that a joke? I replied:

> Damn, was just about to see if you want to
> come out with some *GO* dudes tonight.
> Any interest?

> Where

he texted.

Single word answer, no punctuation; he was not enchanted.

> They mentioned the Marina.

> I see.

He was judging, as if that simple fact of a neighborhood said so much about a person.

> Is that not a good place?

> It's a bunch of rich bros from the peninsula who claim they're from the city and act tough because there's no one real around to beat their ass.

> K. How about the Mission? They also mentioned that.

> Do you not realize what night this is? Halloween? Mission and Castro are going to be dumpster fires. High school kids drinking Puckers and sobbing. Plus gang stabbings.

I put my phone down on my desk. In college, when he was invited to party, he would have simply asked: Will there be women? And even if the answer was no, he was likely coming out, especially if the other option was a movie. And since when was Cole down to watch *Avatar* anyway? I plotted how to respond sensitively.

> Where would you be amenable to going out?
>
> I was probably going to stay home. Why deal with chicks who think they can cut you in line at the bar because they've got their tits out in Laura Croft costumes?

There was a silence. I replied:

> Well, as the local, we'll go to the bar of your choice, where you determine the least amount of offenses are likely to occur. Btw is cleavage that bad?

My phone vibrated:

> No, it is not.

We pushed into Blackthorn after giving the bouncer our IDs. The bar had the World Series pregame on every channel, and it was packed with a clientele that, if I had to guess, cared little about Halloween or anything other than Giants baseball.

People parted to let us through, then zippered closed behind us as we made our way across the sticky floor to the middle of the bar. I saw the backs of Ward and Kevin, who were both looking up at the TVs, chins in hands like cartoon-watching kids. They were in their work plaids, and their elbows were positioned in a way that guarded their personal space. Joe Buck was on surround sound introducing the lineups for Game 4. A camera pan to Madison Bumgarner in the bullpen caused a tide of distress across the bar; people were worried the rookie wasn't ready for the big stage. The Goodyear Blimp gave its aerial view of The Ballpark in Arlington. There was Nolan Ryan, bald and circular, and George W. Bush next to him. People booed the TV, then nodded at one another as though they'd found some criteria for friendship. Madbum walked the first batter of the game on four pitches.

"Blue squeezing him already," Cole said to himself.

I wished he'd spoken louder. I could sense Kevin and Ward twitching for the introduction, and I was searching for an opening, but Cole maintained this divide between them that was made only slightly less awkward by the events of the game. By the third inning, more people had pressed into Blackthorn. Every breath I took was someone else's breath. Hoping to get to the bathroom, or to acquire a pitcher of water, was naïve. Cole hadn't said a word more, to me or anyone else. He was red-cheeked, his sideburns sweat-dotted. Watching Madbum pitch, Cole was probably calling pitches in his head, knowing which were executed, which were mistakes. He was also probably thinking about what it might feel like out there, trying to remember the sensation of calm and focus with a ball in his hand.

"The Giants are such a bunch of misfits," Kevin said. "How they even got here is one of those anomalies."

"So much fidgeting in their batting stances," Ward added. "They need to quiet that down."

They kept looking at Cole, searching for some kind of reaction. Cole held unblinking eyes on the game.

"Pretty eventless game so far," Ward said later.

"It's a tight one," I countered.

Ward nodded with a frown, like he was considering my interpretation as a favor to me. "A lot of double plays," he settled.

At a commercial break, I bought a pitcher and poured glasses as a way to introduce everyone. Cole turned his attention back to the game after we all cheered.

"So how hard did you throw, Cole?" Ward asked.

I tensed. What a boneheaded question to ask him. Thankfully, beer shot up around us like from a blowhole. Cheers blared throughout the bar. On the TV was a slow jogging Giant. When people's arms fell, I saw Aubrey Huff had hit a two-run homer. The bartender rang a trolley bell. Ward and Kevin high-fived, and then all three of us did a sort of pyramid high five. We looked at Cole, our hands paused in the air waiting for him to join. He didn't budge. Moments after, he leaned into me and said, as if it was a conspiracy:

"That ball was titted."

Acknowledge me and no one else; these were evidently his terms for the evening. Ward and Kevin ordered another pitcher. By now, they'd bought three, I'd bought one, and I wondered if Cole would think to grab the next one.

"So how hard did you throw, Cole?" Ward tried again. Cole brought the brown beer Ward had just poured for him up to his mouth.

"This is garbage," he said.

"Newcastle?" Ward asked, then made a face of mild surprise. "Hmm."

A passing gruff man said "Nice hat" to Ward's backwards Mets hat.

"Yeah, it is," Ward said back, and I was unclear what kind of exchange that was. When the seventh inning began with an error, moans spread across the bar.

"Be better, Uribe! You're a vet!" Ward yelled.

The next pitch to Vladimir Guerrero was roped foul. Then with two strikes, Bumgarner threw a dirt ball.

"Make better pitches, Bum!"

Bumgarner struck Vlad out. I watched Cole glare at Ward, who blinked in approval.

"Jesus Christ," Cole said to himself.

Ward and Kevin were proving to be what Cole already

decided they were before meeting them: opinionated turd people. But he didn't even give them a chance, just dismissed them and cherry-picked their low moments—which were ironically the moments that they were trying to appeal to him— as evidence against them. Naturally, he would bitch to me about them later, and there would be nothing I could say to soften his take.

I looked over where Cole had been; he was now pushing toward the exit. I knew from the way he was moving—in the unrushed way of horror villains—that he wasn't just going out for fresh air. He was going home. I decided to let him. Fuck it. I'd been annoyed by people my whole life. Exhibit A: baseball players. Exhibit B: business majors. Did I just walk away from them if they said something dumb? No.

My attitude was reactionary though and quickly faded. I thought of what this night was for him, a visit with his traumatic past, worsened by people who poured salt on the wound. Had our roles been reversed—had I been the one walking out—he would sympathize, I knew. He would come after me, and we would have a conversation.

I closed my tab and walked away at a moment Kevin and Ward were engrossed in the game. I didn't have the bulk of Cole, so I didn't part the sea getting out of there like he had. I had muscles but lacked any assertiveness with them, said excuse me and waited for people to let me through. Outside, Cole was up the block. I followed him into a doughnut shop where homeless were taking shelter from the drizzle.

"What's this?" I asked.

"Two chocolate old-fashioneds," Cole said to the woman behind the glass. She crouched and reached into the rows. "And a milk."

At the cash register, Cole was given change. "How many doughnut holes will this get me?"

The woman took his change and filled the rest of his bag with donut holes.

"That's sweet. Thank you," he said.

"You, sir?" the woman asked me.

"Oh no, I—"

"Get a doughnut, bro," Cole said.

"Dude, I've had six Newcastles and no dinner.

"Don't be rude."

"It's the seventh inning of the World Series. Am I crazy for thinking it's not doughnut o'clock?"

My voice was all intense and repressed like a parent to a child at a restaurant. Cole could do that to you.

"He'll have a bear claw," Cole said.

He looked to me.

"These things are like 25 cents—the least you can do," he said.

"The least I could do? You drank a pitcher of my friends' beer and vanished."

"I'll be walking home. *Avatar* is still on the table."

On slick streets, we passed an occasional trick-or-treater: a girl dressed as a flower and speaking Chinese to her mom, two boys dressed as Giants, their parents listening to the game from a radio. Other than that, the Sunset was dead, a lot of houses with their lights off, the nonverbal of "go away."

"Do you ever wonder how a doughnut shop pays rent in San Francisco, selling a product that's 25 cents?" I asked.

"I used to go there some mornings before school with friends."

We traveled the distance of a few houses in silence.

"Where are your friends?" I asked. I hoped the tone was curious, even oblivious. "Like, who are they?"

"Lot of them didn't move back after college. Some probably settling down wherever they are, probably more affordable. It's weird not recognizing anyone here. Makes the city feel echoey," he said.

My phone vibrated against my thigh; I wondered about the score of the game.

"Except that. I recognize that," Cole said, then hiccupped.

"What?"

Cole paused and put his finger to his ear. In the distance was an aluminum clink. "That. I fell asleep to that noise on Sundays as a kid."

We were approaching a baseball field, where a game was taking place under the lights. From our distance, the field gave off a breathtaking glow, like Earth from outer space. The drizzle had lightened to an afterthought. When we got there, we sat down beside a woman in the stands.

"Extra innings," she told us like it was the chef's special.

"Where are we?" I asked.

"Sunday night league," Cole whispered. "Fiercely competitive lesbians mostly."

I watched a foul ball spin into the air and get hunted down by a woman in jean shorts. Down in the dugout was the buttery voice of Jon Miller from a transistor radio, the chime of bats getting picked up or dropped into a pile. A woman launched a bomb over the left field fence and jogged around the bases.

"How about that piss missile?" Cole said excitedly, digging into his now-splotched bag. He held a doughnut hole out for me.

"I'm good," I said.

I worried about what Ward and Kevin had been saying since I disappeared. And the fact that I lived with and was loyal to someone like Cole must have made me suspicious by association. They were probably comfortable in their judgment, like any two old friends with the same worldviews. I began to dread the questions they would ask me at my desk tomorrow, as well as whatever they left unsaid. When the softball game ended, I was zoned out, thinking of how to explain my going dark on all their texts. The woman who'd spoken to us went down and waited for her beau. The field emptied, the ladies walking out different exits, until all that was left was the field.

"This girl I'm working with. At school," Cole said.

"Dizzy, right?" I asked.

"Dizzy."

That was it for a while. We left the stadium and were walking uphill to our house. We passed a cop lurching slowly down the block with its lights off.

"I don't think she's gonna make it through the year."

"No?" I asked.

"No."

The cop car reached the stop sign, and its brake lights filled the night with red. Then the light went out, and the car cruised on without making a sound. It was like the Sunset skipped the decorations and trick-or-treating part of Halloween and chose to show its spirit by impersonating a Stephen King neighborhood.

"She's got a gun though," Cole said.

"Dizzy has a gun?"

"Not a firearm. Well, maybe. But I mean her arm. She's got an arm."

When we got home, I opened my phone to a "????" text from Ward. I considered all the lies I could tell: sickness, emergency, claustrophobia in the bar. Anything other than "It turns out Cole hated you." I fell asleep with my phone in my hand, having only typed "We."

## (24)

WE WERE INTO month two of our six-month contracts at GO©. I could tell people were starting to press about whether they'd get hired on full time, though they had their ways of acting like they weren't preoccupied.

"I've got a business idea," people said a lot, many of which were centered on organizing meet-ups for people new to the

Bay Area with disposable income, i.e., them. In the GO©-To Cafe, I eavesdropped on secretive conversations about patents and investors. To me, this all sounded like the brain aerobics of people bracing themselves for GO© rejection. I understood. I played those mind games with myself. I was in denial about plenty. But with GO©, my emotions were pretty unconfused: I wanted to work there full time. I'd had my reservations about the culture at the start, the capitalist model, masked by the playful colors and banal body types of the workplace. However, here was a place where I had friends, where my thoughts mattered, and where my work had saved lives.

In my alone time, I'd been practicing for the FTE interview. How I liked the bus rides in the morning, the ventilation, the zen of the dim LED lights. Even the GO© bus stops. There was serenity to the order, the etiquette. People respected each other's space, listened to their music; I did the same. Transplants from Denver, San Antonio, Charlotte, Salt Lake City had their sports teams and little office rivalries. They liked to try restaurants based on Yelp. They were big on food truck events and food fusion—sushi-ritos, kimchi tacos. I was in a fantasy football league in my office, Ward and Kevin and some dudes from New Delhi who knew as little about the game as I did. They taught me about cricket, how you got a running start to pitch and there was no such thing as a foul ball. We went back and forth on which sport was more globally relevant. I dug the perspective. They had weekend games in Foster City, and we liked to say, "Let's play next weekend, like actually this time," and then when the day came, we either said something came up, or we simply didn't contact each other.

I was convinced of the good of GO©. They'd given $10 million to nonprofits and education in the Bay Area and were voted 2010 Top Corporate Philanthropist by *San Francisco Business Times*. Cole ran his mouth about how we were generic, how he could pick people like us out a mile away just from how we ordered a burrito. How we were ruining the Bay

Area. There was a term for us going around—techies. The connotation was cultureless and privileged. It was kind of like "hipsters," in that people cast the label on others as though it immunized them from being one.

How Cole could say we were wrecking the Bay Area was beyond me when companies like GO© gave money and resources to help kids like Dizzy. He said techies "don't get it," and when I asked him to elaborate, he just rolled his eyes. Textbook Cole, being out on something because other people were in. Because stubbornness. He might have benefited from a few more credits in college to expand his capacity for critical thought. Casting judgments without evidence—that made him the one who "didn't get it." Some of the world's brightest thinkers were under one roof at GO©, determining the future, one intuition, one algorithm at a time.

These were the things I'd say if they gave me a FTE interview, which I imagined would be with Audrey.

More than once in the office, Audrey had made some kind of remark about my toned arms. In a parallel universe, it was sexual harassment—maybe? Or maybe not? Either way, if it was harassment, I was down. I also wasn't certain Audrey was heterosexual. Like maybe she wasn't attracted to my muscles but wanted to have them on her body. One morning she asked where I got them. I said pushups and lean meat, and she nodded in a way that looked like she'd never been less horny. But she did have a smirk. I thought this meant she dug our work dynamic. She struck me as someone who liked the upper hand, and maybe I was a workable piece in her puzzle: muscular but unimposing, sharp but malleable.

The morning after Halloween, she was eating a hard-boiled egg, sizing me up by the plant wall. "Out late?" she asked.

"Not especially."

She came up to me so close I saw the light hairs that fuzzed through her makeup. She reached her hand to my hair, fussed with it, then pressed it down on one side.

"You're welcome. Now tell me something interesting. Did you watch the baseball game? Did you dress up and trick-or-treat like a good little boy?"

I told her I had a dream that I was pitching and someone put me in handcuffs. She tsked and tilted her head.

"Kinky."

GO©'s official term for the kind of interaction we'd just shared was "casual collision," and I was imagining a couple different kinds of those with her. A lingering beer fog made me admire her blockish figure as she made off past some computers. I went and got an Odwalla, hoping to run into her again. Afterward, I had a hard time focusing, dragging roads around on a digital map, entering code so GO© no longer suggested a U-turn somewhere.

After lunch I went and sat in the massage chair. In the room with the dim lights and Asian flute and the intimacy of the machine pushing me in tender areas, I daydreamed of Audrey. I imagined us on a business trip to Japan or Beijing, eating dinner beneath a lantern, looking around and recognizing no one, then looking into each other's eyes, knowing whatever we did would be our secret from the world. We would go to our separate hotel rooms after dinner, and then sometime in the middle of the night, I would hear her knock on my door. I would open it. She would slip in, and I would close it behind her.

On the bus home, I closed my eyes. It was weird how sitting all day made you need to sit down. I sighed and thought of what would happen when I got home. Cole would probably ask, "What we doin' for dinner?" like there was no way I could have other plans. And if I did, he would be offended. If I offered my thoughts on dinner, he'd probably dismiss them, just like the other day when I'd floated Kaiyo, this Japanese/Peruvian spot he'd called "basic."

At some point in the night, he was destined to bring up Dizzy, how that day she lied about something or cussed out a teacher trying to help her or threw the free cafeteria lunch on the ground after complaining that she was hungry. There really was nothing I could say; slowly I was learning that. He just wanted his days to be acknowledged as worse, more tiring, more thankless. Even if I said something to cheer him up—"Dizzy will do something to get expelled. Your days will ease up soon enough"—that would backfire. He'd insult me about how life was that simple at GO©, but not at his job, like he was educating me on world realities when I was the one who'd graduated college. And this was where we were as friends: me having arguments with him in my head and getting upset with him when nothing had happened yet. I wondered whether this was common in friendship. Just the thought of it made me want to delay heading home and instead stay at GO©, get a personal flatbread from the GO©-To Cafe, chill with whoever was still around.

## NOVEMBER 2010: A TIME FOR US

# COLE

## (25)

Benson, Dizzy
DOB: 6/21/1994
Ht: 15 in
Wt: 4.5 lbs

6/21/1994
Six weeks premature, narcotics in blood. Withdrawal treatment in ICU five days.

7/16/1994
Blood test results: Pneumonia: positive; Gonorrhea: positive; HIV: negative; Syphilis: negative

3/19/1996
Dizzy Benson recovered from crashed vehicle, conscious, unhurt. Mother Deborah Corvalles deceased, murdered. Father Brigadier Benson taken into custody under suspicion of grand theft auto, possession with intent to distribute. No

known family members fit for custody. California Department of Social Services to intercept to determine legal guardian.

5/14/1997

Second-degree burns on back shoulder and right hand. Foster mother Gloria Brown taken into custody for child endangerment. Dizzy Benson relocated to St. Vincent de Paul for temporary housing.

8/4/2001

Bernadette Clancy appointed legal guardian. Residence 500 Larkin Street, San Francisco, CA 94102. Enrolled at Tenderloin Elementary. Diagnosed dyslexia. Diagnosed learning handicapped. Diagnosed ADHD. Diagnosed emotionally disturbed. Defiant to instruction, inappropriate conversation and social inclinations. Approved for Individual Education Plan, accommodations.

3/10/2003

CTBS standardized testing results: 50th percentile writing, 88th percentile math, 29th percentile reading. Appointed reading therapy.

10/31/2004

Altercation on bus, suspended.


11/21/2004

Stealing school materials (food, calculator) from class cupboard, suspended.


9/12/2006

Fainted in homeroom, 8:45 a.m. Visitation Valley Middle School. Symptoms of seizure, in and out of consciousness, eyes rolled back, foam at mouth. Treated at San Francisco General Hospital for alcohol and Gamma-Hydroxybutyrate. Denies receiving from other party, insists she acquired on her own and voluntarily ingested.


2/28/2007

Missing person reported by Bernadette Clancy.


3/13/2007

Bernadette Clancy terminates guardianship of Dizzy Benson. State places Dizzy with Morgan and Jeanne Fellows, 1403 Flounder Ct, San Francisco, CA, 94130.


4/16/2007

Expelled from Marshall High School. Throwing a weapon (lock) at a student, resulting in a broken tooth, and throwing brick through class in session. Held in juvenile hall for fourteen days. Transfer to Seaside High School. Request for transfer (1-2 hour commute from Treasure Island) not granted.

5/9/2008
Missing person reported by Morgan Fellows.

4/12/2009
Intercepted by SFPD on Market Street in proximity to prior sex trafficker Don Boyle, suspected for sex trafficking.

9/21/2010
Harassment of classmate Grayson Fitsworth.

"IT'S NOT AN official file," Mr. Antonini told me, closing the laptop. "It's also not even close to all of it."

"Whose laptop is this?" I asked.

"Genevieve Dawson. Miss Genevieve. You've probably seen her. She has a caseload of students at a couple different schools, comes to IEP meetings. She's just kind of extra support for our vulnerable population. The girls really take to her elegance, her handbags and scarfs. She's a little proper and standoffish, like Mary Poppins without songs, and it seems to intrigue them. Anyway, I figured you ought to know about

Dizzy now that a month has gone by and you're still showing up."

I was caught up in the economy of words of Dizzy's file. Her life on display, so ruthlessly spare, like the back of a baseball card. Facts, dates, nothing else. What if someone made one of those files on me? How would it read? "3/17/2007—lost strike zone. Never recovered. The end." All the struggle, the prayer, the insomnia, the self-talk, the ongoing urge to slam my head through a wall, the humanity, omitted.

Who was Dizzy, the person, during this? Her dyslexia and therapy. Was she teased? Did her hands go clammy, did her stomach cramp to be summoned for therapy in front of her classmates? Did that little diagnosis make it harder to pay attention in class, make her doubt her own mind? Did it keep her from raising her hand? Did the children watch her sad eyes with some perverse sense of pleasure? The answer was in danger of extinction, known only by Dizzy and probably fading and warping with time, and all anyone had to go off of to learn her story were words in a file—dyslexia, defiant, deceased.

Mr. Antonini placed science supplies on each student's desk for a project after lunch. There were two chemicals, food coloring bottles, and empty two-liters.

"This project got alcohol in it?" O'Shea asked when Mr. Antonini was explaining it.

"A little, yes," Mr. Antonini said.

"I'm bouta turn up."

"O'Shea, rubbing alcohol is poison."

"My uncle RayRay be drinking that," Delfino said. "It's high doses."

"He finna get brain damage," O'Shea said. "Too much chemicals."

"Yup," Majique said.

"My uncle drinks vodka and milk," Grayson said. "For his

ulcer."

Others did not acknowledge nor contest the information, which for Grayson was a social triumph.

"Aye, I seen RayRay the other day," O'Shea said. "They was kickin' him out the liquor store on Third. He had them OG Jordan Breds, the black and red."

"Yup," Delfino said in an unsure manner, as if he couldn't decide if this was a moment to feel proud or sad.

"I was finna ask him where he copped his shoes at, but he had been cuffed up."

"Hi, Miss Genevieve!" Dizzy said to a woman in a long olive coat in the doorway.

"Hi, Miss Genevieve!" Grayson followed.

"Shut up," Dizzy snapped.

"I left my computer here again. I'm so frazzled." She slipped the laptop in her bag. "Dizzy, are we supposed to have our phones out in class? Oh, Dizzy..." Dizzy looked up from her phone where she'd been watching something hectic. "That sounds like violence. Are you watching YouTube fights again? That's a little barbaric, honey."

I watched a bit stunned as Dizzy placed her phone face down without protest.

"What you drinking, Miss Genevieve?" she asked.

"I am drinking..." she turned the bottle, "Honest Pomegranate Herbal Tea."

"What's pomegranate?"

"Look at the label. Have you had one of these before?"

"It look like a clit."

"Psh, this bitch foul!" Majique said across the room.

"How come you don't drink Arizona? That's only ninety-nine cents," Dizzy asked.

"Well, I try to avoid high fructose corn syrup. It's a very sweet ingredient."

"I should stop drinking Arizona then?"

"Should you, you mean? Yes, I think so. Over time, high

fructose corn syrup can lead to bad things like diabetes and high blood pressure. Companies put it in their foods instead of natural sugar because it's cheaper. This allows them to take advantage of kids and people with less education."

Dizzy popped her gum. Her bushy eyebrows furrowed. Miss Genevieve brushed her skirt and slung her bag over her shoulder. Mr. Antonini proceeded with the science project. Everyone chose two colors to put in their two-liters, and they expressed surprise to watch them separate so cleanly like they did.

"OK, guys. Does this remind you of anything?" Mr. Antonini asked.

"No," Grayson said worriedly.

"It's like Nortaños and Surreños," Delfino said.

"Yes!" Mr. Antonini rejoiced. "What we're seeing here is segregation. That even on some basic chemical level, the world is comfortable when it is divided. And that's not what it should be. We need to bust up all that comfort and division and plain color."

Mr. Antonini shook his bottle, and then Grayson joined with his capable arm. Then everyone was shaking their bottles, sloshing the contents into Italian-dressing brown. Miss Genevieve stood at the door with a smile.

"Great work today, Greg," she said and left 10-B.

"Yo name Greg?" O'Shea asked.

Dizzy was looking at the door. When it was clear Miss Genevieve was gone, Dizzy took her phone back out.

"YouTube be needin' slo-mo," she complained. Majique now sat next to her, looking over Dizzy's shoulder. "Clara leave her face open when she reach like that. See? I'ma windmill that bitch. And I hope she wear that ratty weave."

She let out a breath of consideration.

"I'ma study this before they take it down," she said.

"Yup," Majique said. "You know they finna. Cuz that girl titty pop out at the end."

Beneath Dizzy's seat was a Doublemint wrapper ripped into confetti. Her foot bounced as she looked out the window. To me, she had the face of someone trying to mute out the weight of her thoughts. There was a wish in her expression, and I interpreted it to be that she was alone, in a different moment.

She grabbed her bottle, looked at its radiant division, swirled it around. When the bell for the end of school rang, she left the project on her desk and took a right out of 10-B, against the current of students. Dizzy in her baggy hoodie, with her frayed hair, each strand looking to be in a conflict with itself, walking out the exit no one else ever used.

"Dizzy, hold up!" I called.

# ISAAC

## (26)

---

Subject: ATTN RED BADGE EMPLOYEES

GO©-To Cafe is being relocated to BLDG 3B. Access will be restricted to upper management and those with white badge clearance. This also goes for rooftop yoga. But we've still got plenty of hot and cold cereals, sandwich items, and a salad bar, plus the yoga room in PQR2 gets great sunlight. I might actually choose it over the rooftop.
Keep on keepin' on,

Audrey

---

AS A TEMP, I had up until this point enjoyed access to the GO©—To Cafe—sushi, tapas, oysters on the half shell, beer on tap, always open, always free. White badges were engineers and whatnot—the ones really making all this magic happen. They got earthquake kits. They could go see the campus nurse or dentist. And now there was a building exclusively for them, which initially made me laugh, the optics of a progressive company like GO© having a whites-only building. But I chose not to see it as the warning sign some of my colleagues did; to me it was just motivation to be converted to full time.

Ward hit me up on AOL AIM instead of GO©'s internal messaging system. This meant the topic was serious, something he didn't want to risk being snooped. It was funny to be adults with respectable jobs, but using screen names from puberty.

> WARDn'tYouLikeToKnow: Dude you guys
> hear about Bila from accounting?

I knew of her. She caught the bus in the morning at the Wawona stop with me. We'd never spoken, but I had heard her soft voice speaking on the phone and watched her stomach grow in the last month. From what I'd gathered, she was having a girl, planned to name her Ava. But now that Ward mentioned it, I hadn't seen her in the last few days at the bus stop.

> LuckyNumberKevin: I heard she went to
> management about health services for
> pregnant temp workers or something.

> WARDn'tYouLikeToKnow: Poof. She gone!

> SirIsaacTheGreat: Damn. I just realized
> there's been someone new at the bus stop
> where she would stand. Lightweight
> Twilight Zoneish. Some dude with red
> stubble and a messenger bag. Looks like
> his name would be Zeke or Linus.

If Ward or Kevin were nervous about our workers and amenities curiously vanishing, they didn't show it. On AIM, they soon moved on from Bila and brought up moving to the Marina when their lease soon ended.

WARDn'tYouLikeToKnow: Higher price point for sure. But the value is commensurate, maybe even disproportionate in our favor. In my eyes, you can't put a price tag on the 3 B's. Beach...Blondes...Bomb Sushi. Lol jk. But seriously.

LuckyNumberKevin: It's just a healthier lifestyle.

WARDn'tYouLikeToKnow: Plus there's a *GO* pickup in the area.

LuckyNumberKevin: Dude, Ward. What about a three-bedroom??

WARDn'tYouLikeToKnow: Whoaaaaa. You have my attention.

LuckyNumberKevin: Isaac, you're not on a lease in your Sunset apt are you?

SirIsaacTheGreat: Nah. I just pay month to month. Cash.

WARDn'tYouLikeToKnow: That's so Chinese.

LuckyNumberKevin: Lol. So there's nothing binding that is keeping you there?

SirIsaacTheGreat: Basically, just need to give my 30 days.

WARDn'tYouLikeToKnow: Dude...

LuckyNumberKevin: You don't want to be in the Sunset for your early twenties.

WARDn'tYouLikeToKnow: Yeah bro. Loogey-ville USA.

LuckyNumberKevin: Why don't we hit Marina tonight? Do a little recon...

SirIsaacTheGreat: I'm down. Gimme ten minutes to wrap some things up.

We wound up at the Tipsy Pig where some Oregon State alums were barking at a game on the TV. We were on our third round, starting to pull our phones out and browse Yelp for dinner.

"Don't look now," Kevin said. "I believe Audrey just entered."

This news sobered me. I hoped it was her. I hoped it wasn't her. I snuck to the bathroom and splashed water on my face, then dried it so as not to come off looking like a chronic sweater. When I came out, Ward and Kevin were shaking hands with Audrey's two friends. Audrey saw me from across the bar and threw up her hands.

"Look at this motley crew!" she said. "I assume you are out enjoying a libation to expand the mind for the sole purposes of GO© project discussions."

"Exactly," Kevin said.

Ward took out his phone.

"Don't mind me, I'm just Googling, 'are you allowed to rage with your boss on a Thursday?'"

"At ease, soldiers," Audrey said. "These are just some belated birthday shenanigans. These gals were out of town last month for my real thing."

"How inconsiderate! Can we buy your first round to smooth things over?" Ward asked. "Wait, let me Google if that's allowed."

I needed Ward to crank down his little fucking wind-up toy motor already. I could tell Audrey's laughs were charity at best, and I was trying not to be associated.

"Well, our res isn't for another forty-five. Be our guests," Audrey said.

"Where you guys eating?" Kevin asked.

"Gary Denko," one of her friends said.

"Dammmmmmnnnn," Ward said. "Oh, you fancy, huh?"

"What're you guys drinking?" I asked, needing a way to exist in this conversation.

"I'll have a pear martini. Laura does gin and tonics, and Estella likes pinot."

"That's wine?" I asked.

"Right, slick."

The drinks took long enough for me to drink half a pint. After I served her friends, Audrey shifted toward me.

"So." She held out her glass. I clinked it.

"I didn't know people actually drank martinis outside of predictable movies," I said.

"Much to learn, young grasshopper."

"Is that from a predictable movie?"

"Maybe. What are we even talking about?"

"I don't know," I said, suddenly frightened.

"I have a question for you."

"OK."

"How did you know that Cake answer? On my birthday, the one Ward got wrong. I thought it would stump everyone."

"You underestimate your workforce."

"Yeah. But come on."

"I watch too many movies and listen too obsessively to the music in them."

"Then what are your favorite soundtracks?"

"Unfair. I couldn't answer that before your reservation. How about yours?"

"Unlike you, I'm not scared to answer a question. I don't know about, like, original scores and all that stuff. But my favorite soundtrack is probably *Romeo and Juliet*, the nineties one with Leo and Claire Danes."

"Great call!" I said, which felt too excited, so I tamed it with, "Favorite song off it?"

"Oh, god. Now that is unfair. I mean, 'Lovefool' comes to mind, but that's the easy choice."

"Of course."

"But that Garbage song can't be overlooked either. I used to dance to it in the mirror in high school and feel like a rebel. Shut up, don't tell anyone."

"Lips sealed. Those are my two favorite from that soundtrack too. And honorable mention goes to the Radiohead cut."

"Yes."

With talk of *Romeo and Juliet* in my mind, I imagined tucking the lock of hair in front of her eye behind her ear.

"For what it's worth, you said you're not into original scores, but the love theme to *Romeo and Juliet* is beautiful," I said. "It was written by an Italian composer, Nino Rota. He also did all the music for *The Godfathers*. If Gary Denko's the kind of restaurant with violinists serenading guests, you can request it tonight."

She smiled. "Noted."

I attempted to check my watch suavely. "Another?" I asked. "Oh, OK."

"Hey, easy, tiger!" Ward called from the corner. "That's not how you get a raise!"

With fresh drinks, Audrey asked if I'd ever wanted to be a musician, and I said I had, that I wanted to have a band with the emotional depth of Smashing Pumpkins and listenability of Third Eye Blind, with a voice somewhere between Silverchair and Bush, but that I watched too many music videos and spent too little time learning guitar. I wasn't positive, but I thought I detected her to be a few millimeters closer to me since finishing our first drink.

"How about you? What did you want to be?" I asked.

"I was a super-original girl and loved horses. But for me it wasn't just because every other girl had Lisa Frank stationery. I could pet a horse's leg for hours. I wanted to ride them. We didn't really have much money, but my parents bought me some equestrian lessons once for my birthday. When those ran out, I was pretty hurt. They said I could maybe qualify for a scholarship for the team, but it turned out I was too short."

"I thought it was advantageous to be dwarfish for that stuff."

"That's jockeys, dork."

I wondered how there could possibly be a horse-riding hobby that required tall people and one that required short.

"Even though I had to stop riding, I kept going to the stables to feed them. My dad would buy a bag of apples and take me after work to Half Moon Bay during rush hour. I still go sometimes. There's even one horse who's still alive from all the way back then. Good old vintage Herbert."

"His name is Vintage Herbert?"

"No. Just Herbert."

She looked at me out the side of her eye, somewhat concerned.

Ward announced, "We gotta get a photo!"

"Then it's time for dinner. With the violinists," Audrey said.

"'Love Theme' from *Romeo and Juliet*," I said. "Alternately called 'A Time for Us.'"

"OK, I won't remember."

She paused.

"But I will remember our conversation."

She walked away before I could respond, which was probably better. Ward got the bartender to take the picture, our arms by our sides, all just sort of standing as though unsure of our relation to one another. It was like a photo at a charity event around one of those huge checks. We said good night, and they were gone.

"Dude, did Estella have a thing for me, or am I making this up?" Ward asked.

"Was probably just the first time anyone pronounced her name with a lisp," Kevin said, putting his arm around his friend. "You might have just been picking up on her sssssssshhhhock."

"I think there's something to be said for all the questions she asked me."

"There was curiosity," Kevin awarded.

"I'm about to post this shit," Ward said and sat down with his phone.

I went to the jukebox and inserted a few dollars. Scrolling through all the bullshit—the '80s hairbands, all seeming to be named after poisonous animals, plus a band called Poison—I realized I'd forgotten about Audrey's earlier email. She'd sent all of us a pretty terse communication informing us that our privileges as temp employees had been reduced, and yet none of us seemed to mind or even remember. In fact, at that moment I found myself feeling sympathy for Audrey; these clearly weren't her decisions, but she had to disseminate them and maintain rapport. It must have been uncomfortable for her to run into us like that, and I felt bad to have been the cause of any awkwardness she might have felt. I searched the jukebox for "A Time for Us." It was there on a "Best of Nino Rota" album. I decided not to befuddle the Thursday night sports bar with opera, and instead played "Fancy" by Drake, a song I didn't much care for. I looked at Ward, who didn't seem to remember referencing the lyrics minutes before to the ladies.

"That was wild running into them," he said. "Would it be unwise for me to drop subliminals to Audrey about Estella?"

"Early signs indicate yes," Kevin said.

"What can I say?" Ward said, cracking his knuckles. "I'm a risk taker."

They looked for a restaurant, and I resolved to not waste another token on Drake. We ended up at Delarosa, a pizza joint with five stars and three dollar signs. Ward kept looking at the picture he'd just posted on Followed, typing what I had to assume were replies to comments. Surrounding us in the restaurant were similar lively groups—young people with nice shoes and hair and healthy, strong teeth showing each other things on their phones as Arcade Fire played in the background. At 11, Kevin suggested I just crash at their spot instead of figuring out the whole splitting a cab thing.

"Yeah, dude," Ward said. "We got a Keurig for the a.m."

Cole texted around midnight:

Where you at? You good?

I replied:

Gonna crash at K&W's.

I thought more about Kevin and Ward's proposal. Living

with Cole had always been nice because it was only $700 a month. As a roommate, he was low pressure. I knew his mind, anticipated his words. He did the same with me. We could go hours in silence. He really didn't associate with anyone but me, which strengthened my sympathy, made me protective of him. And of course, there was still a warmth in me when I thought about Fresno State, back when everyone in the world wanted to be his friend and it was probably uncool to be mine, but he came and talked to me anyway. I had been a ghost until then.

Our neighborhood, the Sunset, had its charm too, its little par-three golf course where the last hole overlooked the ocean. You could hear the monkeys and peacocks from the zoo. There was a good arrangement of Eastern food near Irish pubs. But our spot was getting suspect. It had mildew, a leak in the kitchen sink that was creating black mold, and when we emailed our landlord about it, she asked if we'd tried duct tape. The heater was broken and the living room window permanently ajar, so with November here, Cole and I watched ESPN with quilts across our laps like we were terminally ill. We stopped emailing our landlord, affected by some juvenile worry that if we pushed the matter, she would evict us.

And Cole was starting to change. I sort of dreaded going home to him. He spent his idle moments scrolling through nothing on his iPad or his phone. To watch him do it made me tense. He shot down all my ideas that would get him out of the house. Live music at the Warfield or the Fillmore. Bike ride on Mount Tam. Trivia night somewhere. His job tired him out, working with who he did, but not once had I heard him consider quitting or finishing school. He preferred resentment. A couple weeks earlier, when the Giants won the World Series for the first time in San Francisco history, parties spread into the streets. Roads shut down, "We Are the Champions" played from people's balconies as down below the whole city danced and hugged and sprayed champagne, and when stores ran out of champagne, people sprayed forties. Cole was nowhere to be found, hiding in our house like it was '44 Berlin. A few days later was the parade, and GO© rented out two suites that overlooked the Civic Center, where one million people jammed in. Folks were hanging off street posts and tree branches. There were chants and speeches and bands. But Cole refused my invite.

"None of those people are even Giants fans," he said. "They're not even from here."

"And?"

What he meant, I didn't know. But it was multipronged, I felt. He thought all these people were stealing something, undeserving of it. What it was, he hadn't really ever articulated. The culture? The fun? The roads? The pursuit of happiness? It seemed to be his philosophy more and more that people enjoying themselves were unforgivable. And, a little more often than I was comfortable, he insinuated that I was turning into this kind of person. But at the same time, he wanted me around so he could tell me, and so he wasn't alone.

> You still have that bucket of baseballs?

This was the next text I received from Cole after telling him I was staying at Ward and Kevin's. It was a day later, which I found childish and intentional. The delay communicated much, and I wasn't in the mood to be made to feel guilty.

> Ya, why?

I replied.
He took a while to respond.

> Do you have an immediate need for them?

he texted back.

These balls—I'd almost forgotten I had them. At Fresno State, when it had finally been clear to me that I would never play, I started to steal them from the program. Anytime I retrieved a foul, instead of returning the ball to the game, I would pocket it. Or sometimes after catch, instead of putting the ball back in the bucket, I put it in my bag. Inventory wasn't kept. Balls got lost all the time, then were replenished. It was factored into the overhead of a baseball program. No one suffered. Some balls were porcelain white, and others had baked in the sun and begun to yellow like old newspapers. This thievery was not petty revenge against Coach Lonnie or Fresno State. Rather, my thought was, when my time with baseball was done, I wasn't going to have collected much in terms of memories or accolades, so this was something tangible, a takeaway from a time in my life. Now those balls were in a bucket beneath my bed, untouched since we'd moved to San Francisco. I texted back:

> I mean, obviously no. Why?

> Would you be devastated if some of them disappeared?

> Dude. Can you be less cryptic? You're texting like a shitty TV mystery.

I kept waiting for the new message alert, but got nothing. I knew this was his way of telling me I was being dramatic. But if you looked through the texts, clearly it was him. I stuck around after work in Silicon Valley and got a few beers with Kevin and Ward. When I got home, the air in the house felt thinner. Something told me to go check my room. I lifted the bedsheet that hung to the floor. My bucket of balls was gone, and there was no Cole.

# COLE

## (27)

DIZZY PAUSED AT the door after I called her.

"What," she said bluntly.

"Where you going?"

Dizzy wasn't trying to play games. She knew I knew what she was about to do.

"OK," I said. "It's just...there seems to be, like, a three-strikes thing going on with you. And you've got two."

"Nobody told you to worry about me," Dizzy said.

"I mean, yes. They did."

"You hella starchy."

"I don't know what that means, but you're probably right."

She turned to walk through the exit.

"18 Wedemeyer Street," I said.

"Who?"

"It's a place. Go there. Instead of your fight."

18 Wedemeyer was a place I'd encountered by accident one night in high school. I'd overheard a girl in math class talking about a house party she'd been invited to. Her first language was Russian, and she seemed to have a maturity about sex beyond the rest of us freshmen. She was thin in a way that didn't imply eating disorder, but youth, and she was after men who liked girls in pigtails. She was often seen getting into BMWs after school and being driven off. So when this girl—Dasha—gave her friend the address to this party, I concentrated harder than I ever had in school. I told my then-friends, JV football types with buzz cuts, No Fear T-shirts, and

Jordans. Dudes who had secret hard drives of porn. We devised alibis to tell our parents, skimmed liquor from our parents' cabinets into Natural Geyser bottles. Cognac mixed with rum mixed with tequila mixed with vodka. It tasted like punishment. We met at the bus stop at Stonestown. Of course we didn't have phones to direct us, no GO© maps then. This was something of a hopeless quest. The bus took us through the Richmond on Park Presidio. We peered out the rain-studded window and got off where we thought the party might be. This became a night of us wandering Clement, lost. We went to a Green Apple Books, pretended that the book titles amused us.

Back on Park Presidio, beneath the canopies of cypress trees, our shoes soaked from unmowed grass, cops drove past us, slowed down, and then kept driving. I wondered—was this being a teenager? Was this friendship? Would my weekends fall into some sort of pattern of this, roaming somewhere on the outside of things, hearing my own footfalls on sidewalks at night? This was when we found ourselves in the parking lot of an immense, abandoned complex at 18 Wedemeyer Street. Several light posts along the perimeter illuminated grids of clean windows on a brick building.

"What is this place?" I asked.

"Re-ha-bil-i-ta-tion Clinic of..." a boy read. "I think this is where people with AIDS go."

"Fuck this!" a kid yelled, this apparently being his breaking point. He picked up a rock and fired it. Right through a window it went, clean swish. The shatter was perfect, wet sounding. An alarm sounded, and at once we were running, our night finished. The boy who threw the stone boasted as though he might have a career in something.

Ten years later. I was telling Dizzy to take the address down. "18 W-E-D—"

"I can spell, bitch," she said.

"No one can spell this."

As she turned to leave with the address on her hand, I knew she wasn't sold on my proposal. Shit, I wouldn't have been either if a borderline stranger gave me a mysterious address lacking context.

"Dizzy! Just one more thing," I said.

"Bruh," she said.

I'd about run out of time with her, and I was grasping. "That girl you're about to fight? Clara?"

Dizzy tapped her foot.

"I watched her fight on YouTube over your shoulder. She looks like Rick Ross. You're about to get your ass beat."

"You ain't listen to no Rick Ross. You be doin' Zumba classes."

"OK," I said.

She gave a busted look, trying not to smile. "Aye, I'ma tell her you said that though."

"18 Wedemeyer. 5 p.m."

## (28)

THE COMPLEX WAS still an expanse of Walmart proportions, only now it looked more abandoned than before. Many windows were knocked out, and elaborate graffiti ballooned across the walls, leaving very little original brick to be seen. Hanging on a lamp by a shoelace was a naked doll.

This was a shitty idea. No way Dizzy was coming. Even though it was clear to me that she didn't want to fight, she couldn't just no-show. That was worse than getting stomped. And if the administration got wind of this fight, or if it popped up on YouTube, Dizzy was done, and it felt like there was a riptide force pulling for this outcome, if not tonight, eventually.

Suddenly the graffiti was bathed in new light. It slid down and was soon aimed at me, making me squint. Approaching me, a police car. I had a Pavlovian instinct to run, but I had too much inherent fear of the law. The brakes squeaked, and the car loomed in front of me. I heard the distant walkie-talkie static. The door opened, and a woman leaned out onto her feet.

"How we doin'?" she asked. It was a low, gruff voice, but not like the prick cops who picked on teen skateboarders to feel power. She turned on her flashlight, and now there were intersecting beams, like NBA games during the lineups.

"What you got in there?" she asked and aimed the light at the bucket I was sitting on.

"Baseballs," I said.

"This is a defunct hospital."

"I was going to meet someone."

"Here."

I nodded, then she nodded, as though such an answer confirmed a suspicion.

"Do you have some identification?"

This felt less like a banal misunderstanding. The cop's partner must've gotten a weird feeling too because the passenger door opened and another figure came into the night. I was now being seen as a threat, and the people who found me threatening had guns. That thought made me scared to tell them the truth about this night. It never occurred to me when I told Dizzy to come here that I could wind up in cuffs, which I'd been in exactly once before.

It was a frat party at Stanford. My friend from high school, Jack, had invited me. Jack was observant, made jokes that were both wise and spare, never seeking the spotlight. He had that adolescent discipline to do ecstasy but also ace stats tests and graduate a year early. Jack had been unable to get me on the guest list but told me the names of some of the douchebags he knew from the fraternity for me to pose as. When the first name I tried was declined, I got back in line and tried the next name. By my third attempt, the Polynesian security guard knew my face and seemed amused by my hustle. But a campus security guard was also present. He'd likely noted my sagged pants, crooked SF hat, XXL white T, and decided I was no Stanford student but a trespasser, and potential threat. So he told me to get off campus, that he had a taser and wasn't afraid to use it. I ignored the warning mostly because I didn't take a cop in shorts seriously. I got back in line and gave it one more shot at the party, and the security guard let me in with a smirk.

The party featured much rejection for me. I wasn't any girl's type. Walking around, I found Jack nowhere, stole rare beers and Jell-O shots when possible. It felt rather refreshing to be unproven here. Girls closed themselves off to me and literally said "Ew" to their friends. A perspective, a reminder, of how subjective and illusory my Fresno fame was. At some point, a girl was amenable to grinding with me on top of a table for the duration of a G-Unit song. She rested her head on my collarbone. I locked my lips to her salty ear. This was promise, I thought, but she drifted off in a polite way that hurt more than straight-up rejection. When the party ended, girls huddled together outside and smoked cigarettes, and I found Jack talking to a friend about getting gyros.

"Well, look who it is."

I turned around, and there was the campus security guy.

"Didn't I tell you what would happen if I saw you again?"

His tone was like something delicious was afoot.

"You're about to tase me?" I asked.

Stanford students gathered and watched.

"I'm a student of Stanford, and he's my guest," Jack told him. "I registered him in the campus security office."

"This may be true," he said. "However, that no longer holds weight in the event that campus security orders him off campus. Which I did at 10:24 p.m."

"Aren't you supposed to fight crime?" I asked.

"How about I escalate this?"

The man tugged me toward the campus security car, a Hyundai with an orange siren. The cold metal of the cuff bit at the side of my wrist. I expected the man to open his shitty little door and tell me get in. But there was a pause, and I heard him sigh.

"If I uncuff this kid, what are you gonna do?" the cop asked Jack, suddenly sounding defeated.

"He'll leave, like you said."

"Fine."

The keys clinked.

"Get out of my sight," he told me, possibly something he'd practiced in a mirror.

Black students voiced how the night would not have concluded so fortunately had I been black. White students nodded knowingly and angrily, as though they knew even better than the black kids. It was their way of reconciling privilege, it seemed, acting beyond informed, then getting gyros and talking about it safely among themselves. This was my history with the law, up until now.

"I was driving down Park Presidio," the policewoman said, "and I saw a young lady veer off into bushes, right about sundown. I pulled up beside her, and I recognized her. See, Dizzy here, she's my girl."

She pointed to the silhouette standing at the passenger side door.

"She and I go back to my probationary days on TI. So I ask her what's going on, and she tells me she's meeting someone. A man. And that sounded a little off. I mean, look around. This isn't a wholesome place to meet a man."

"I already told you, he my teacher...sort of," Dizzy said exasperated.

"Hey." The officer raised her hands in surrender. "You ain't in trouble."

She turned her flashlight at my ID.

"So, Cole Gallegos. I'm Officer Padilla. Let's talk."

"I'm Dizzy's paraprofessional at Seaside High School. She was going to fight a girl after school. I knew that if she got in any more trouble, she was going to get expelled. I was originally hired to at least try to keep her out of trouble."

"Bruh, your voice shaking like a brittle ho," Dizzy said.

"Anyway," I said. "A few weeks ago, I discovered that Dizzy has a strong arm. Accurate and strong. She's used it before, dangerously. I know she's been expelled from other schools for it."

"I remember," Officer Padilla said.

"She's got anger, obviously. I told her to come here because breaking stuff feels good when you're mad, so I guess my thoughts were a few broken windows in an empty building was worth a kid's future."

"Dizzy, do you feel safe around this man?" Officer Padilla asked. Dizzy burst into laughter. Officer Padilla went to her car, I assumed to run my background.

"You got me fucked up," Dizzy said quietly to me. "Bringing me to vampireland for some sports."

I listened to the nearby traffic. A motorcycle revved, then died out, leaving us in silence. I thought of some responses to Dizzy, like *Forgive me for trying to help*, but knew she would annihilate such a sentiment.

"On your feet," Officer Padilla said, stepping out of her car. "Your info checks out. So..." She shrugged. "Why don't you pop open that ball bucket?"

"Actually?" I asked.

I had this worry I would open it and, like in some nightmare, there would be bricks of heroin.

"Might as well. We came all this way. Here, I'll go first," Officer Padilla said.

"She finna scrub," Dizzy said.

The building was a considerable toss, probably 150 feet, especially difficult in a cop uniform.

Padilla crow-hopped, her baton swung. The ball spent very little time in the air before skidding down the parking lot and stopping at the foot of the building.

"I'm not sure that dispelled all my rage and angst," she said. "But it's the thought that counts, right? Perhaps you should show us how it's done, Dizzy. Did you play ball growing up?"

I offered her a ball, expecting her to refuse it. Instead she situated it in her hand, bobbed it as though trying to guess its weight.

"My daddy coached when I was a kid. They got hella baseball fields on TI. People don't know that. That man got me one of those pink gloves wit the squishy ball. But I said I don't need no squishy ball. So we played with a ball like this."

"I knew your arm wasn't new to baseball," I said.

"I'd be pitching against the older kids."

I could imagine her gray pants pulled up to the knees, the cloggy look of kid cleats. I imagined her staring down a batter twice her size, blowing bubbles, yelling at him to step his ass in the box, drilling him in the elbow, not saying sorry.

"Why did you stop?" I asked.

"Because."

Dizzy put her head into her jacket, the same North Face as always.

She was crying. I didn't know whether to feel proud or sorry for having coaxed out this sincerity. Perhaps this was breaking down a wall between us, crucial if I ever hoped to become the person the school had hired me to be. Maybe this night had been a good instinct after all.

"Dizz, honey?" Officer Padilla said and stepped toward her.

"We don't have to talk about it," I said.

Her face stayed in her jacket. I figured since Dizzy had broken down, it was a good time to be vulnerable myself, to level with her for the first time as well.

"You probably don't believe me, but I guess it might help to know that I actually used to—" Dizzy's face popped out, smiling.

"Fuck naw, I ain't never played no baseball!"

"Right," I said.

"Everybody just stand around looking gay."

I sighed.

"Well, Miss Smartypants, are you going to have a throw?" Padilla asked. "At least make something out of this tanking night?"

Dizzy was laughing.

"Aim for the third floor windows," I said.

Dizzy narrowed one eye in measurement. I got the sense this challenge out-dualed her ongoing itch to fuck with me. Gravel crunched as she got her footing. She lunged. Her arm went straight back to her ear, quarterbackish. Her finish was poised, the flick of her wrist thick with confidence. The release, questionless, doubtless—as simple as it should be. This ability, the easiest yet most overlooked part about pitching—the letting go—vanished, just like Dizzy's ball. Into the night. It had that trajectory I'd always worked toward. It had late life and rose the farther it went into the night.

There was a deluge of glass, like a fallen chandelier. A cathartic sound. Dizzy took another ball and whipped it, this time without focusing. The ball dove through a window on the second floor.

A couple more tosses, both slapping against the brick.

"Hey, what's up with all these balls?" Officer Padilla asked, inspecting them like produce. "They all say different colleges."

Usually, I would be inclined to lie, but something stopped me. It felt weak to orchestrate this night and then retreat from all its truths.

"I was a ballplayer in college," I said. "A projected first rounder."

The cop said nothing. Maybe I wanted to talk about it finally, and I wondered if Dizzy was responsible in a way for that evolution.

"But I stopped throwing strikes. I forgot how, essentially."

"Oh yeah?" Padilla asked. She seemed to be trying to gauge if this was supposed to be funny. "Like, something happened to your head?"

Dizzy tossed a ball up to herself, processing my words, not fully checked out. "How much money was you about to have?" she asked.

"According to all the baseball dorks? Like a mil," I said.

"A *mil*? That's hella fabricated."

"Nope."

"And they ain't pay you nothin'?"

"Now the schools pay me to be your role model." Two moths sparred in the beam of the headlights.

"You ain't break your arm?" she asked.

"Arm was healthy."

"You wasn't starving or didn't catch no case?"

"No."

"So it was like, you just gave yourself problems?"

"Basically."

"You hella white for that."

Dizzy flipped me the ball.

"Just throw one. I'm tryin' to see this train wreck."

The last time I'd held one of these balls—NCAA official, with the raised stitches, the firm hide, Western Athletic Conference stamp—was the day I ran away from the game.

## (29)

I'D BEEN FEELING better about my start against Army. Time worked that way for me, allowed me to return to a healed self, or at least mind. It didn't feel like delusion. Spiritually, I felt close to turning a corner on this thing. Then came a text from Coach Lonnie:

> Practice @ 1 today

It was a recent revelation, Coach texting the players. Some intern had set up his phone so he could text the whole team at once. The texts were rife with typos and dated words that delighted the team, like when he texted:

> Be @airport @ 630. Wear Collared Shit
> and Keds,

and the team held a competition for best reply.

I'd always liked Coach Lonnie for his oldness. It shielded him from being artificial or falling victim to trends and lingo. Sometimes after practice when everyone was fixing the field, Lonnie would wrestle around. Guys would put him in a headlock, and he'd emerge all red-faced and put his hands up like the fighting leprechaun. Once, when I was pitching in Hawaii, we broke open a 0-0 tie in the seventh with a grand slam. Our whole team burst out of the dugout, fists raised high like we'd sacked a village. Green Gatorade cups of water streaked through the air.

Our next batter got drilled in the back in retaliation. Of course, when I went back to the mound the next inning, I glided one mid-nineties into a Hawaii dude's ribs. That's just how it was and always would be. The benches got all huffy and spilled onto the field, and Lonnie was the first one out of the dugout, pointing a stubby finger at Hawaii, snarling out of the side of his mouth. After, in the dugout, you could see his eyes glint in the leather of his face. It was like a part of him had been fed. You wanted to be led into conflict with him. You wanted to have a beer with him and hear unfiltered stories. And with my breakdown getting worse with each start, I'd begun to feel like I was personally letting the man down. And he was the last guy I wanted to do that to.

"Did Coach move practice to 1?" I asked Isaac on the couch.

"Lemme check my phone." He went to his room. "Nope!" he

called. "Still 2:30 as far as I know."

"Weird," I said to myself.

The field was empty when I got there. I thought I saw someone in the dugout, but it was a bucket. Down in the bullpen though, I spotted Lonnie and Murray, the pitching coach, waiting for me. Murray was OK, I guess. Like most assistants in college ball, his objective was to be hired as a head coach somewhere. This meant he kissed Lonnie's ass. That way, whenever he applied for a job, Lonnie would give a good recommendation, which would go a long way, given how long he'd been in the game. With Murray focused on his future, he didn't make connections with our pitching staff. Didn't lift with us or join us on team jogs like younger coaches were known to do. He didn't have our backs. On the road, if we were out past room checks, he would rat us out to Lonnie. If it was late in a game and our starting pitcher was giving it everything he had, he wouldn't vouch to let us stay in to get that last out. And recently, with me feeling nerves just from the sight of a baseball field, it would be nice to have a pitching coach I felt I could trust.

"Hey, kid," Lonnie said as I approached.

Murray sat there, looked at his watch. Something felt off to me, like in the Mob movies when a guy gets called for an impromptu car ride.

"Wanted to have you throw a pen," Lonnie said, then clapped his hands, which felt like a weird gesture, like it might rush me past any suspicion. I looked around the empty field.

"How many pitches?" I asked. "My start's tomorrow."

Lonnie hinged his teeth side to side, figuring out his words.

"We're gonna let you loose here. As many as you need."

"Need? For what?"

"Just to get some work in."

This political vagueness was not Lonnie's strong suit; he sounded almost like he was guessing. The fact that he was bad at this type of thing was what made me choose to come to

Fresno in the first place.

"It's a simulated pen," Lonnie added, as if pretending there were batters in the box made this a special opportunity. Clearly they'd axed my start against Army. I could tell from the melancholy of Lonnie's eyes that the coaching staff felt they couldn't win with me on the mound anymore.

"You want me throwing into a net?"

"Of course not. Murray will catch you," Lonnie said, and Murray sprang to his feet and jogged to the bullpen home plate.

"Jesus Christ."

"Let's just get some work done today. How 'bout it?"

I started with warm-ups, the short tosses facing Murray head on. They went smoothly. I backed up some steps, and the throws started to cook, burrowing at Murray's chest. Then I was 90 feet out. In my follow-through, my drive leg went up and planted softly like a bird landing. I was out at 120 feet. I even went a few throws without thinking about it.

When I got on the mound, home plate looked so close. That was a sign my arm felt good: when the catcher seemed as close as the fingers in the Sistine Chapel, and I could just let go of the ball and it promptly made the glove pop. As the pen got under way, I could tell I was jamming Murray's thumbs; he kept taking off the glove between pitches, shaking out his fingers. I hoped one of my sliders bounced right off his nuts. This was the Fuck You feeling that had always been a part of my success but had magically vanished. After thirty pitches, I had thrown twenty-five strikes, each one sounding like the crack of a whip. I took a break, toweled off my forearm, squeezed a stream of water into my mouth. Lonnie was off talking to someone on the phone.

"Looking good," Murray said. It was an annoying tone, like I'd made a wise move against him in a board game. "Coach wants you in the stretch for the next twenty. Then finish the pen with situations."

"I've thrown a pen, thanks," I said as Murray walked back

to the plate. "Hey, Murray."

"Yeah."

"Why am I here before the rest of the team?"

Murray looked at Lonnie, ensuring he wasn't within earshot. Murray could've ad-libbed all kinds of answers. He could have said, "Coach wanted to give you all the time you needed, didn't want you to feel rushed." Something like that. I wouldn't have believed it, but still that would've been better.

"Coach, he..." Murray began. "You know how silly he gets. He's old-school. He's a mystic." Murray chuckled. I smiled to go along with whatever this was supposed to be. "Coach was getting worried that if other players saw you...you know...you might give it to them. Or something."

I flipped the ball to myself.

"Just some boomer silliness," Murray said, then jogged back to the plate. It was probably his idea in the first place.

Normal Cole would have told Murray, "Bro, don't ever say 'silly' again." But I was no longer Normal Cole, or normal anything. My mind was now spinning from what I'd just been told. Two players had just arrived to practice. They were figurine-sized in the distance, wearing shorts and cut-offs, shaking their protein shakes. These two were always early to everything: to the bus, the continental breakfast on the road, study hall. It was a trait I'd never understood, I guess because I never had to prove myself. It had always been a world, at least these last precious years, that operated on my time.

"Let's kick back in gear, boys!" Lonnie said, fresh off the phone. "I don't want Cole to get cold." He sounded anxious to wrap this up.

"Twenty more pitches!" Murray said, spitty from inside the mask.

But it no longer felt like twenty pitches. The news that Coach saw me as a contagion had taken over my mind. Standing on the mound no longer felt like I was taller than everyone else, but like I was on top of a tipping world. I dug my spikes in, began my delivery. I drove; my arm dragged, and out came a floater. Murray didn't so much as lift his glove. The ball flew over the netting behind him, landed near our home dugout, and rolled right up to my teammates who were lacing up their cleats. A spoon of bile rose to my throat.

"Another ball," I said, held out my glove. Murray scanned the dirt. Lonnie underhanded a ball to Murray, who relayed it. I packed the ball into my glove, gripped it until it rug-burned. I wanted it to feel like it had always felt, before my mind was conscious of failure, of irony, of how we're all one molecule, one thin membrane from the swift deterioration of the mind. It was only a fucking baseball. It went where you threw it. All you did was look at your target, and that's where it went. Simple. I exhaled a breath, then exhaled another. With my spinning head, I tried to look at Murray's glove. It floated around like the Cheshire cat. The next pitch bounced ten feet in front of the plate.

"Shelf it!" Lonnie blurted. "Shelf it."

I stuck my glove out. It shook like the rest of me. Murray held onto the ball; he'd heard his orders.

"Enough for today," Lonnie said. "You threw great."

"I threw sixty of eighty," I said. "You fucking smiling, Murray?"

"Go down, see Mike," Lonnie said, stepping in between us. "He'll set you up with the med balls, the bike. Get a nice sweat going, ice down."

"I don't need ice."

"Great to see you back throwing strikes."

It didn't sound like Lonnie, but someone rigid from acting school auditioning for Lonnie. The coaches walked off to the dugout where more of the team was gathering. Isaac was down there, I could tell, sensitively taking all this in, trying to look oblivious. What was I supposed to do now? Walk past the whole team, like the guy who gets laid off and has to box up his things in front of his colleagues with dignity?

I hoisted myself over the hip-high chain fence of left field. I knew it would draw the eyes of my teammates, who now felt like strangers. Everything felt like a stranger. A baseball was like a stranger. Class felt like a stranger. Consciousness. I curved toward the parking lot like I'd done so many times, only this time it was my last.

## (30)

IN THE FANGED San Francisco cold, I felt the eyes of Dizzy and Officer Padilla. This was something I needed to do now, before the vertigo and loss of feeling spread. I crow-hopped. My arm sliced through the night. The ball left my hand and disappeared, as if sucked into outer space. Padilla and Dizzy waited for the ball to hit off the brick or make a sweet avalanche of glass. But it was not seen or heard.

"I think you threw it clear over the building!" Padilla said.

"You just woke up one day and forgot how to do that?" Dizzy asked.

"Pretty much."

"How come you could do it now?"

"I'm not in front of a crowd, I guess."

"I knew you was white, but this like green smoothie white."

"You keep mentioning white. Yips are not a race thing," I said. "You know who else has yips? Charles Barkley."

"Then that dude white."

"Charles Barkley?"

"Yeah."

"Uh, no."

"I see the makings of a great friendship here," Officer Padilla said.

Ball in hand, Dizzy sized up the building. Or maybe she was looking beyond the building, beyond wherever my ball had just arced, via some innate itch to be better than. This time she crow-hopped, too, having observed me. As we watched the ball sail out of her hand toward the building, the lamppost went out and visibility went dark. Dizzy, Officer Padilla, and I didn't move. We waited to hear the crash, or anything. There we stood, holding our breaths.

# (31)

ON MONDAY, I took an early bus to meet Mrs. Melvin before school started. She went pale at the sight of me outside her door.

"I'm not quitting," I said.

She placed her hand on her sternum. "Don't scare me like that," she said.

She had gotten a haircut over the weekend, reduced it to something PE-teacher short. Her coffee machine gurgled to life.

"When you hired me, you told me this whole thing with Dizzy was a race against the clock, that we needed to get her a diploma before she did something to get expelled."

"I did," Mrs. Melvin said noncommittally.

"I think I found a way to help those odds. It might be a little outside the box. Or, more like, outside the school."

I explained Dizzy's arm strength vaguely, omitting the questionable instances I'd seen it in action: the cracked window of 10-B, our off-campus rendezvous with a cop.

"You want her to play catch," Mrs. Melvin said.

"Yes. No instruction or drills. Just catch. Breathing."

She nodded and tilted her head, a visual of her weighing mind. "There are issues of fairness and safety," she said.

Couldn't everything be, depending on the lens? How about being a foster kid? Dizzy's past, and holding her to the same standards as someone with two present parents, reliable meals, safe neighborhood? What of that was fair?

"Do you think she could have aspirations to join a team?" Mrs. Melvin asked, paving paths in her head.

I laughed.

"My thoughts are that catch itself could be like a form of therapy, not a means of achievement or Hollywood story."

"Play time is a crucial element for youth," Mrs. Melvin said. "You know, they took recess away from kids in Chicago Public School District in the early nineties. From kindergarten through high school, some students never got a break in fresh air. Some schools out there still operate like this, twenty years later. I don't need to tell you the state of Chicago Public Schools."

"Exactly," I said, hoping this topic did not linger, or any other topics that might expose how little I knew about anything. I knew catch. Or at least I once did.

"Structured playtime correlates with better literacy scores and more classroom engagement. Especially for hyperactive students," Mrs. Melvin continued. She was forming the nicely packaged adult iteration of my idea, doing the work my head could not. She windshield-wiped some papers around her desk.

"I *will* say, I don't think much is lost academically from her taking leaves of absence from Mr. Antonini. No offense to him."

"The kids respect him," I said. "Enough to keep showing up. That says something."

"Bingo. As I'm sure you've picked up, with what some of our students go home to, school can't be about homework and worksheets and due dates. Don't make me laugh. It needs to be a place where they can just go. To feel safe. It needs to be a system that cares, doesn't target or assess."

"Then have I made you an offer you can't refuse?" I asked. Mrs. Melvin smiled like now she was awake.

"You have a glove for her?"

"I do."

"Well, I've watched school districts make some pretty poor decisions on behalf of its students before. I don't think this could wind up any worse, right?"

# (32)

THE NEXT DAY, Pierre, a skinny San Francisco State environmental studies student was standing in front of the students of 10-B. Mr. Antonini as well as other Seaside teachers had received an email from SF State's science department offering their grad students to come and present on biomes, and Mr. Antonini hadn't given it a second thought.

"We're going to respect our visitor, right?" Mr. Antonini asked. "We're going to keep our phones away? No outbursts? We're not insulting each other? We're not insulting Pierre?"

Pierre gulped.

"They're all yours!" Mr. Antonini said. I was counting down the seconds before someone blew Pierre up for his Airwalks.

"OK, guys," he began. "Let me ask you all a serious question. When you think of the desert, what plant comes to mind?"

"My girl pussy be a Venus flytrap," O'Shea said, possibly a lyric. Mr. Antonini pinched his chin at the statement, as though it could have hidden merit.

"Well... There actually is a crazy thing about the Venus flytrap," Pierre responded, already having to call an audible on his lesson. "You know what it is?"

"*What*?!" O'Shea mocked.

"Pff," Delfino laughed.

Dizzy popped her gum. In moments, she might walk out on Pierre midsentence. I had both gloves and balls in a backpack at the front of the room, ready for our first catch.

"You would think a plant like the Venus flytrap, a plant that eats animals with sharp teeth, would be at the top of the plant kingdom, right? Like the shark or lion of plants. But! You'd be mistaken. The Venus flytrap is a surprisingly fragile plant. Easily defeated by the elements. If it doesn't have the right soil or sun, or especially if it receives too much water, it wilts and dies."

"That's like a baby dying from too much love," Majique said.

"That was quite insightful, Majique," Mr. Antonini said.

"Shut up."

"Orchids, too," Pierre persevered, "are another beautiful plant that dies if it receives too much water, or love. Another lesser known plant called the money tree plant dies with too much love."

"That plant retarded," O'Shea said.

"Put that plant in 10-B," Delfino said.

The walk to the field was five minutes. Dizzy had the hood of her jacket tugged well over her head, and she looked down at the pavement, trying to remain anonymous on this fieldtrip. There were rushes of cars on Bay Street and silences as we waited at stoplights. Women carrying rolled-up yoga mats passed us. A man in front of his apartment spoke on the phone about a merger in his pajamas. Up ahead at the field was a group intensely engaged in Frisbee. At the field, Dizzy squinted in the gray bright of the near-coast. Before we began, she told me the only reason she was here was to get away from Pierre. I said that was a perfectly fine reason.

I released the first toss gently. Dizzy swatted it into the grass out of self-preservation. Two sparrows circled her ankles, wove braids with their paths. They looked both in quarrel and harmony.

"You listened to Kendrick Lamar?" I asked.

"No," she said.

"Kanye?"

"He a spoof, bruh."

"Who do you listen to?"

"I keep it Bay."

"E-40?"

"I mean. He goofy, but he a real one."

"Nickatina?"

"He kinda on some weird shit. You bringin' up all the old-timers."

She threw the ball right to my chest. That she had never played baseball didn't compute for me. Her throw also showed me that as cerebral a game as baseball was, it favored those who hadn't had a chance to overthink it.

"Ya Boy," she said.

"Who?"

"Ya Boy. Ya Boy got bars."

"Who is my boy?"

"The rapper named Ya Boy, stupid ass."

Dizzy got out to about 90 feet. She shook loose her jacket. I noticed she stuck her tongue out when she threw, Jordan-dunk-ish. In the stands, a glass bottle rolled down the steps where a crispy man lay shirtless. The calamity of the bottle made me realize minutes had gone by without worrying that my disease would resurrect. My lungs filled with salt and fog, and when I exhaled, I still had wonderful, intricate feeling in my fingertips.

"Do you know why the sparrows are doing that?" I asked.

"What?"

"Those two. Zipping around your ankles."

Her toss had a mild and pretty arc with effortless zip.

"It means there's a nest nearby and they're protecting it. It's their way of distracting predators."

"This boring," she said.

"Just think. Somewhere in the Philippines, a child is drinking puddle water, learning math by drawing numbers in dirt."

"So?"

"So..."

I twirled the ball in my hand, then dug for a slider grip. How long it had been since I'd conceived of throwing a slider. I whipped one at her. It changed direction midflight like something military. Her eyes grew wide, and she leapt. The ball kicked past her ankles.

"So that," I said. She took her time walking after the ball.

"I thought you couldn't do this shit no more!" she called.

Low morning fog was thinning like tugged cotton. Over in the stands, a pigeon flapped at the homeless man. He threw up his hands and yelled. Then he snagged a banana peel in a territorial manner.

"He up there havin' turf wars wit a pigeon," Dizzy said.

## (33)

"YOU GOT MONEY?" she asked the next afternoon, clenching her fist open and closed. I had a Velcro Indiana Pacers wallet, won at an arcade as a kid, which I just kept using until it became ironic. As I got older, I never wanted to spend money on a new wallet because I was broke. So that was what I was working with. I pulled it out and braced for a crushing insult from Dizzy, but none came. Her eyes were red and fleeting, and her tone distant. I opened the wallet. There were four dollars and some ancient change.

"I thought this job supposed to pay you," she said.

"You all right?" I asked. "You seem, like, disturbed."

She sniffed.

"I ain't disturbed. That's you, chief."

"How much do you need, and what's it for?" I asked.

We were at the park now. Nannies encircled the playground

where children somersaulted around, swung on swings. Catch didn't seem on the horizon today, so we just walked through the thick outfield grass, picked up smells of lunch from Chestnut.

"Someone ever punch you in the face?" she asked.

"Like square in the face?"

I tried to craft a response that preserved any respect she had for me, but was honest: no. My silence was enough.

"I fuckin' hate takin' one to the face," she said. Her breaths sped.

"Not cause of the pain. Like it's a fight, adrenalin take pain out the equation. But it don't stop you from that stunned feeling. Nose get wrinkled, make you look like you cryin' even though you ain't. And it always be in front of hella people wit they phones. And you wanna just scream, like, 'Timeout for a minute, bitch.' But ain't no timeouts."

"You're fighting Clara today, aren't you?" I asked.

She looked at me like I was an idiot.

"And I ain't had no lunch."

On Van Ness, we passed a couple apartments with awnings and fire escapes zigzagging up the windows. They conjured images of buffed linoleum lobby floors, a nice receptionist in a hat greeting visitors. The smells of the lunch hour on Chestnut came with the breeze.

"I mean, do you have to?" I asked.

I knew trying to Houdini another escape for her was futile; the fight was happening. I had choices here, all of which left Dizzy or me in some kind of danger. If I didn't give her money, she wouldn't eat, would fight feeble, the thought of which broke my soul a little worse than the thought of her fighting period. I could do the adult thing and alert Mrs. Melvin or security, but Dizzy had been here playing catch with me these past few weeks, which was evidence of her extending herself for our friendship; it felt like a version of myself I couldn't accept to narc on her after we'd reached a point where she trusted her real self with me. So here I was on a quest for sustenance for a high school girl to be in her best fighting form. We passed the deli where kids got egg bagels in the morning. Four bucks wasn't going to cut it there. It was getting comical, the prices for food in this city: $13.99 for a crepe.

Even the cutty cash-only joints were getting the memo that new people were moving to town who would drop ten on some toast. It was like some social experiment that would be revealed in a groundbreaking *NY Times* article someday.

We entered the corner store on Van Ness where I first saw Dizzy. We worked within my budget.

She held up items in the aisle, and I gave either thumbs-up or thumbs-down. Nestle Ice Cream bar: thumbs-down. Cup Noodles: thumbs-up. I added a Clif bar and a coconut water. Dizzy poured hot water from the black thermos in the coffee section into her noodles. She sprinkled the change into my hand, and I used it to get a fifty-cent tube of peanuts. Every calorie mattered. I recalled yesterday when I told her Filipino girls were drinking puddle water to imply other people in the world had steeper hills, worse odds stacked against them. I cringed, like when you see pictures of yourself from your regrettable phase in middle school. Dizzy stirred the broth.

"Don't tell nobody." She breathed out the steam of her first bite. "About none of this."

I nodded.

"You hear me?" she said.

"I hear you."

## (34)

THE NEXT MORNING I sat in 10-B watching the traffic on Bay Street. Dizzy wasn't in class. Different buses squeaked to a stop, off-boarded students, blasé in their lateness, and old fishermen with rods sticking out of buckets like antennae. After first period, a bus arrived, and when it moved along, Dizzy was sitting on the bench.

I crossed the street and sat a neutral distance from Dizzy at the bus stop. A passerby would think she and I were strangers. I kept my gaze on the face of Seaside, its nauseating cream color smogged over time by traffic. A sharp gust came from the coast behind us, but Dizzy didn't appear to feel it. She drew in a long breath and let it out through her nose, then put in her earbuds. There was a thin scrape across her forehead, and her lip was puffed like an allergic reaction. Without inspecting her, that was all the aftermath I could gather from yesterday's fight.

A Lincoln Town Car, shiny and black, pulled up to the school entrance, and out of the back seat came Kate Scott. I knew her because I'd read an article on her in the Seaside newspaper in which she discussed her senioritis on recruitment trips for volleyball and how the decision to accept a full ride to UCLA was the toughest of her life. I'd seen her in the hallways manipulate all flirtation from the boys into something harmless and platonic. It was like this time period was a cute precursor to marrying a brain surgeon and having vacation homes. She texted with her thumbs as she closed the Town Car door.

"I hate November," Dizzy said at last. "Hella frosty."

I thought I heard the absence of background sound. Dizzy had turned off her music. I wanted to ask her something, like if she was thirsty or if she was OK. But she probably wasn't trying to be the subject of any more pity than she had to.

"You ever take a limo to school like that?" she asked.

"Nah."

"*Brady Bunch* bitch."

Kate Scott looked over her shoulder at us on the bench, perhaps sensing our conversation.

"How about you?" I asked.

Dizzy had something of a dreamy expression as the Town

Car slid through a green light and drove off. It was as though she were imagining herself in its leather seats, eating a cold Pop-Tart, pouring juice into a chandelier flute as students gathered around and cupped their hands against the window to see who was inside.

When we got to class, Dizzy got her folder and a pencil and started on her math worksheets without being asked. It was peculiar to see, even the slightest bit unnerving. I waited for her to snap out of it, break out a lighter and set it all on fire. But she kept on, like she was taking being a student for a test drive to leave the person she'd had to be yesterday. No one in 10-B called out her wounds. The boys didn't grill her about the fight, but let her be. Before lunch, she turned in her blue folder, which was spiderwebbed with creases.

"I thought that folder was lost months ago," Mr. Antonini said. I was looking over the math work when Miss Genevieve walked in.

"Knock, knock. Just checking in on our scholars."

The lunch bell rang, and Dizzy quietly walked past her. I watched Miss Genevieve survey the color on the side of Dizzy's eye. When the rest of the students emptied 10-B, she voiced her disappointment about Dizzy and her fighting, phrasing it as dangerous, not to mention primitive. I disliked how sure people were when using logic that made sense in their lives and applied it to others. It was convincing if I wasn't careful.

"I don't think the fight was what she wanted," I said.

"She made a choice. She has so many dedicated people, like you, trying to help her, pull her up. It's a choice," she said almost cheerily. I couldn't determine if this was a disagreement or a lesson.

"Dizzy seemed to be on task today," Mr. Antonini said diplomatically. "No disruptions, no confrontations."

"Here," I said and held out Dizzy's folder for Miss Genevieve. "Check it out."

"Oh," she said and stepped back, creating what felt like a

delicate standoff. "No, thank you. This may be TMI, but my husband and I are trying to get pregnant, and I just want to be a bit mindful about germs and..."

"All right," I said and handed the folder to Mr. Antonini, who shrugged, opened it, and stamped her work with his signature stamp: "HOLLA!"

In the daylight at the ball field, the banana-yellow of Dizzy's bruised eye was glossy. The questions I had—What happened in the fight? Why did you do the math work?—I pocketed. My encounter with Miss Genevieve and seeing Dizzy 20 feet away, tossing the ball to me with her hanging face, left a weight in my chest. I was in the mood to blame someone for something.

"You ever have an extra-shitty teacher?" I asked eventually. "Like, who's the worst teacher you ever had?"

"Man," she said and seemed to brighten at the topic. "It's so many different kinds. It's teachers who hate kids, and then teachers who's just dusty. Teachers who be doing the most to be your friend but don't nobody respect them."

"I understand."

"When I was a freshman," she said, "it was a teacher kinda like you. Like, he was a teacher, but he wasn't a teacher-teacher, you know?"

"A para."

"A what?"

"Nothing."

"This man said he was a doctor or something, said he had a PhD. He'd be wearin' doo rags, hella different ones. O'Shea ask him where he got his PhD at. This man said the streets. Dude was on some phony shit. Talking about we was kings and goddesses, wit all the potential in the world if we put our minds to it. Grayson sitting there lookin' like a toad, gettin' told he could run for president. I'm like, wait a minute? And he didn't teach us nothin', just sat on his phone, snapping selfies wit us."

"Selfies?"

"Wit the doo rags. We wasn't havin' it."

Dizzy was having to call to be heard and taking time in between throws. It gave her rhythm, let her fill her lungs with air. I watched the ball get bigger as it left her hemisphere and sailed toward mine, heard its hiss crescendo into my glove. It had been weeks since my disease occurred to me. If one or even two balls were to slip, Dizzy wouldn't care, perhaps not even notice, or she might insult me with the same severity of any of my other flaws, and I would be at ease, which was probably why I'd been humming perfect tosses with her.

"Anyway, this man started coming to school late," she yelled. "His eyes bulgin', spittin' Tupac verses to himself. Our principal was like, that's a wrap."

"Was he on drugs?"

"Not even. I dunno. Anyway, we show up one day, he ain't there, and it's an old bitch instead. It was old-bitch musical chairs up in our class for months. There was this one who really got on my nerves. It was her *first* day. But she telling me get out my books or we going to the principal. I'm like, 'You even know how to get to her office?' She all, 'If you don't do your studies, you'll work at McDonalds.' I threw a milk carton directly at that ho."

"Full?"

"Yes. How you 'bout to throw an empty milk carton?"

We looked at each other like we'd encountered the kind of riddle people scale mountains to ask monks. She pinched her chin and laughed.

"That carton exploded, right atop the bitch head!" Dizzy fell into the grass, did snow angels.

"Eventually we was wondering about that dude," she said. "Mr. PhD of the streets. Took us hella long to find him 'cause none of us could spell his white-ass name. But we seen him on Followed and creeped his ass."

"What was his name?"

"George. George Heimlich or something."

"That name frightens me."

"When we found him, and mind you he already been fired for hella months, we seen that he had posted that day, a selfie from our class, talkin' about 'Here I am doing my part making a difference today.' We scroll down, and we see he been posting some positive message everyday since his ass been fired! Sayin' stuff like, 'It never feel like work to have such a positive impact on the youth.' All of that. And he out here getting so many comments. There was pictures with me in it! Like this man had been taking selfies to prepare for when got canned."

"You guys report him?"

"*Did you guys report him*," Dizzy mocked, as if there were no clearer giveaway of our different worlds.

"OK. So what happened?" I asked

"This boy Carlos made a fake Followed page. We took hella measures against our man George. Blew his ass up. I don't even know if that page still exist. I ain't checked it in hella long. 'Cause Carlos moved away."

Dizzy took off her glove and reached into her black coat. She pulled out her phone and began to thumb, an industrious expression on her face, which turned into a smile.

"Bruh." She laughed. "Here it is."

## Followed

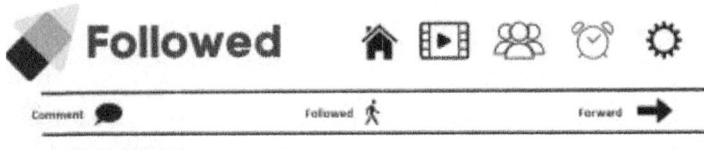

"Did you hear about the rose that grew from a crack in the concrete? Proving nature's laws wrong, it learned to walk without feet. Long live the rose that grew from concrete when no one else even cared."
—Tupac Shakur
Inner city special education has its peaks and valleys, in many cases the students have not been given opportunities, and frankly, love and support. But we out here PUTTING IN THE WORK! For now, break time, lol.

**Comments:**

### Eduardo Hughes
Your commitment is inspiring and contagious!

### Geraldine Moore
When I have kids, I'm trying to have them go to whatever school you're at! LOL 😊

### Melanie Johnson
As an educator I feel the same way. Bless us all for the work we do.

**Geoffrey O'Harrison**
I've been thinking of a career change, something more fulfilling. You seem to have figured it out. Life is about giving!

**Veritas Satire V**
Bruh is you takin a dump?

**Veritas Satire V**
Aye you wanna come clean and tell the people you is terminated from this job?

**Veritas Satire V**
THEN I WILL. ATTENTION FRIENDS AND FAMILY OF GEORGE GEORGE BEEN FIRED FROM THIS JOB FOR MONTHS. HE AINT ON NO BREAK. HE UNEMPLOYED. PERIOD. YALL OUT HERE LETTIN THIS MAN FEEL GOOD ABOUT HIMSELF. WHAT HE NEED IS A JOB INTERVIEW, AND A SANDWICH.

---

## (35)

"WHAT'S UP WITH the name?" I asked.

"My boy Carlos was lookin' for other words for truth, 'cause we was exposin' it. We seen veritas. Then we just spelled it backwards and looked that up. Satire. Which meant making fun of people. And it was on after that."

"I gotta say, this is good," I said as we walked back to school. We never spoke about her fight.

By the time I got home, afternoon fog had rolled in. Windshield wipers were on in passing cars. Gusts vroomed against our living room window. Before giving in to the pull of an afternoon nap, I flipped off the cover of my iPad. The screen never ceased to feel futuristic in its sterile, unsmudged glow. I checked Followed. Views from offices, epiphanies I didn't read, someone I didn't recognize getting engaged. Followed recommended a row of people I "might know." And there was someone eerily apropos. It was one of those moments that made you wonder if we were being surveilled, our conversations eavesdropped on, our thoughts read, without our knowing it. Who was to say Followed, or something in my phone, wasn't listening to me all day and churning the algorithm to produce this friend recommendation:

**Followed**

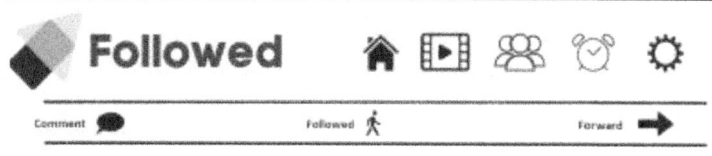

Comment | Followed | Forward

**Genevieve Dawson**
Lives in Sausalito, CA
From New Haven, Connecticut. Employed at SFUSD
Married to Shiloh Wang, Co-CEO @ Wishscape
Interests: Bon Jovi, brunch, cuddle time with Bruno my Great Dane, believing in a better future!

---

I fell asleep.

# ISAAC

## (36)

AT GO©, LUGNUTZ was the term for those who drove the goofy cars or walked up and down streets pushing dollies strapped with cameras, collecting data. They, in addition to all the civilians utilizing the "Report Issue" feature in their GO© apps, were responsible for hundreds of issues in my queue each day. A past version of me probably would've felt like a hamster in a wheel, but the work-inspired me? We were apprised weekly of miracles made possible by our hours at GO©. Most recently, a woman in labor made it to the hospital on time in Papua New Guinea, having been redirected to a more efficient route by our app.

When I wasn't buried, I had been hatching a business idea. This was not to pursue if GO© didn't hire me. Rather, it was meant for GO©. I hadn't told anyone, but steadily I had been adding layers to it, like a reverse Jenga. GO© wanted to expand by leveraging its mapping software and innovation into other industries. For that, I knew they were looking for more than just hard workers. GO© valued innovators. And since the day I was recognized for my work in saving a family in the snow in California, I'd been thinking, what's stopping me from being an innovator?

My idea: to use GO©'s mapping software and navigation technology to create a faster emergency dispatch system. Currently, 911 connected you to a dispatcher in your area, who triangulated your location, then sent out a notice to whoever was nearest, and then someone headed that way. But what if the 911 call triggered the response, cutting out the minutes lost on explaining your emergency, being told to calm down, that someone would be there shortly? What if the second the emergency call was answered, everything was instantly in motion? Maybe press 1 for cops, 2 for fire department, 3 for emergency. I didn't have that part figured out yet. But in an industry of seconds, my idea would shave seconds, even minutes, from the average call-to-arrival time.

Beyond a quicker response, there was an equity aspect that I felt made my idea just as attractive: What if GO© aggregated data of cities and neighborhoods in America with historically longer wait times for emergencies, places like where Cole's students were from, and derived an algorithm that ensured calls from those areas never waited longer than the national average? Disrupting the status quo of emergency response like this would expose and attack systemic disparities. This was not farfetched for GO©, given its history of brazenly making lofty concepts reality. And the fact that the core of this business model was philanthropy, not money, was what made it so potentially lucrative.

I wanted to bounce my idea off Ward and Kevin; their professional minds were more polished. But I wasn't ready for anyone to tamper with it or, worse, steal it. So I was waiting for the right time to reveal it: my FTE interview, when my contract was up next month.

I went home for Thanksgiving. Riverside was how I'd left it: one-story law offices, megachurches, and substandard pho. At the dinner table, my parents proudly and inaccurately explained GO© to my aunts and uncles. When I got back to San Francisco, I went to Ward and Kevin's apartment instead of to see Cole. He and I hadn't texted much over the break other than about Fresno State's football game, a 59-0 loss to Boise State. I worried about him in that empty house, what went through his mind, how he passed his time. But Ward and Kevin's place was warmer. Their pantry had more than earthquake rice. It was only a block from the Page, which served Pliny the Elder on tap.

"Dude, we gotta pull the trigger on a Marina flat," Kevin said.

We were eating take-out shawarma in their living room, watching the Niners smear the Cardinals on Monday Night Football. Ward griped about Alex Smith throwing 2-yard passes on third and eight, and Frank Gore screwing his fantasy season. Kevin took bites so big he had to breathe through his nose. It was hard to believe he tasted what he was eating. I wondered what I looked like, what people concluded about me when I ate.

"Me and Kevin were researching. December across the board is the best time to lock in a lease. East Coast rent is about 5 percent cheaper in December because no one wants to move in the weather. But you gotta think people operate by that general scale everywhere during the holidays, right? Property values are starting to spike near tech bus stops because the moneyed want to live there. And landlords are moving out their existing tenants to accommodate them."

"Moving as in evicting?"

"Sure."

"Is that good?" I asked.

"I mean, it's change. It happened in the dot-com boom. Cities…change."

That statement hung in the air. It sounded profound initially, but then I wasn't sure what he meant, and I didn't think he knew either. It was vague enough that were I to ask him to clarify, he could reshape it to fit the temperature of the room.

"Either way, for us, all signs point to get in now," he continued. "Somewhere a few blocks off from the GO© bus stop. I've seen some spots off of Gough and Filbert."

"Were people evicted there?"

"That I don't know," Ward said thoughtfully.

"How do you know they wouldn't evict us someday?" I asked.

"I mean, they're going to see GO© in our employment section, so they'll know."

"Know what?"

"That there's no one to replace us with. We are the apex tenant."

I had to admit, there was an ironic persuasion to Ward; his decisive tone helped neutralize the goofiness of his lisp, and the goofiness of his lisp softened his colonialist tone. What he was saying felt logical. Being in my mid-twenties with a good job meant I should be living where things happened, where days had sun, where ceilings were high and windows were big, where girlfriends—maybe someone like Audrey with *Sex and the City* sensibility—would find it acceptable to wake up. Kevin and Ward already had so much furniture I wouldn't need to buy much, maybe nothing. With Cole, our situation still felt college-y. Sticky floors, space heaters in our rooms, take-out containers left out so long they became part of the decor. He didn't seem to have ambitions of ever moving either. Same with his job, which paid him shit; he never mentioned pursuing a new one or figuring out college, how to mitigate his lack of higher education. He just moaned from the couch as though it were destiny for the world to screw him. We were adults now. I was not obligated to his chronicles of woe. Dude didn't even reply to my texts half the time.

I had a text to him typed in my phone and was staring at it, unsent. I needed to get this over with. Next weekend GO© was renting out a brewery as a fundraiser for local indigenous tribes, and I had invited Cole a while back, before we started to grow apart. There was a possibility he'd show up still, and if he did, I needed him to know my housing plans beforehand. He was not someone to have things sprung on him.

My phone rested on my chest, my finger keeping it up like a field goal holder. Then I began to fall asleep. The phone slapped my chin, and in my fumbling, I accidentally sent the message:

> So I might be moving to the Marina at the end of December. Kinda just happened all fast, but figured I should tell you ASAP so you're not totally screwed roommate-wise.

It was a tangle of words, meant to appear like all this was out of my control, like if it were up to me, I would stay. I used to be someone who apologized and admitted when wrong. Baseball kept you accountable like that. GO© had caused a shift in me though. I'd picked up a language so apologies didn't happen, because apologies meant fault, and fault meant weakness.

I felt a bruise of dread for Cole's response, but told myself this was good for him, that these situations made one emerge not wounded, but calloused for the inevitable disappointments of life. It felt like something my Dad would tell me as a child, and I was turning out relatively OK.

The next morning, there was no response. Of course there wasn't. This was Cole we were dealing with. No discussion, just seal off from whatever hurt you and leave everyone tense and confused.

## (37)

WARD WAS IN his "Froyo Is A Food Group" t-shirt which I'd seen him wear on festive occasions like this. He, Kevin, and I caught a cab on the earlier side, took Oak to Octavia, and let the freeway hug us into Bernal Heights. It was a charming neighborhood; I'd never been. On a windy hill with panoramic views of the city, I got an aerial reminder of how small it was. Streets and neighborhoods crammed against one another, like a cracked-open crystal. Dogs whirled around with a million-dollar backdrop that their owners took in with coffee. Down Cortland Street, a Mexican produce market, and near that a health food store, the kind that smelled like spices, where you could buy raw beans and grains from a container.

We walked down to the brewery, just before the 101 overpass that canopied two tents and some men sitting outside them on lawn chairs.

I dug the Chex mix at this brewery, very cheddar forward. The beer selection was appropriate for the time of year. Dark beers for the cold weather, a cranberry Kolsch, a selection of IPAs made with juniper and elderberries, with their history of importance to the local tribes explained on the menu. For the month of November, the brewery was giving half the proceeds from those beers to the Native American Health Center of the Bay Area.

Dinesh and Patty, two teammates on Operation Land Lens, rallied in ping-pong, while Kevin and Ward squared off in a game of Connect Four. I watched Audrey flutter table to table, munching, working on a half-pour of something. Having rented the section of the brewery where the TVs were, we had autonomy over what was played. Audrey had brought some old

DVDs, arranged it so *The Goonies* was on mute while David Bowie played across the brewery. Sometime in the early afternoon, people began to enter in 49ers jerseys. They tentatively scanned the scene, checked the TVs. I watched the bartenders shake their heads, point toward our party, and shrug in a "my hands are tied" gesture. The Niners people left slowly. The elderberry IPA had an understated musk that had me going back to it. I was feeling more and more assured that Cole would not be coming. There was little about this scene that would draw him in regular circumstances, but now that I'd dropped the apartment situation on him, there was even less. It was a relief not to have my two worlds do their awkward handshake again. I went to Audrey, who was having a moment with *The Goonies*.

"Wanna play Connect Four?" I asked.

Her eyes lingered on the scene, kids basking in piles of pirate treasure by candlelight.

"I call black," she said, then flashed her black fingernails like a cat scratch.

"I'll get it set up," I said.

Over at the table, Ward and Kevin were still playing.

"What is happening here? You've been at this for like an hour," I said.

"Best of eleven," Ward said, flipping a piece between his finger and thumb.

"Let me on this game really quick. I'm playing Audrey."

"When we're done," he said.

"Dude, he's playing Audrey," Kevin said. He eyed their game in progress. "I just committed it to memory. We'll resume after they play."

"Fine," Ward said, flicking the release, and all the checker pieces avalanched.

"So," Audrey said after seating herself. "Have you strategies?"

"I was just wondering that myself."

"You've got to be weighing whether it's better to defeat your boss and impress her with your intelligence or let her win so as not to upset her."

She raised her eyebrow at me.

"Your move."

I dropped a red piece arbitrarily. If my senses were accurate, Audrey was not invested one way or the other in the outcome, just the preliminary mindfuckery. It felt like even if she got four in a row, she might not notice.

The pieces piled up into a red-and-black mosaic. And through the empty circles, I saw a familiar movement from the corner of the brewery. It passed from one hole to the next until it stopped, right in the middle of a hole, looking at me through it. I couldn't look away or blink. It was like sometimes when I slept and I knew I was awake, but my body was paralyzed.

A black checker dropped into my view, snapping me out of ocular entrapment.

"Any questions?" Audrey asked. She cracked her knuckles.

I registered her four diagonal black pieces in a row, but my mind was now elsewhere.

"If you'll excuse me, my shame is too much to bear," I said and scooted my chair out.

"Connect Four freed up?" Ward asked Audrey.

"Abso-lizard," she said.

"Nice!"

Nearing the counter, I confirmed Cole with longer hair and a hoodie I didn't recognize. He sat on a metal stool, foot twitching, reading the overhead menu. It felt like the drunk uncle had shown up at Thanksgiving. I wanted to ask him why he came. Other than to fuck up my day, guilt trip me. Of course he would say because I invited him. Some cheeky shit like that.

"You made it," I tried.

He sniffed out a laugh, like I had already failed his realness test.

A man in a 49ers hat came up to the counter and patted Cole

on the back. They recognized each other but couldn't tell from where, I detected.

"Don't you take the twenty-eight in the mornings?" he asked.

"Yes!" Cole said. They bro-slapped hands. "Isaac, this is my bus driver in the mornings."

I extended my hand and shook his. The man asked the bartender where the Niners game was. I shuddered. The bartender pointed to the corner of the brewery, said the party over there had rented the space and with it access to the TVs.

"Oh," the man said. "And they ain't playin' the Niners?"

He sounded less appalled than fascinated. He and his friends left.

"Good luck," Cole said to him, then turned to me.

"Yeah, I know," I said.

The bartender asked Cole what she could get him, and he said he needed a minute.

"You're mad at me," I told him. "I get it. Let's talk about it."

"What's there to talk about?"

"I mean, you came all the way out here, to what. Not talk about it? Let's try to be adults."

"Just get me a beer."

"What kind?"

"I don't know. Wanna talk about being adults? These beer names, fuckin' Lucky Charms Pie."

"He'll have an elderberry IPA," I said. "You'll like it. It's like Sierra Nevada."

We spent a half a beer in silence. Cole reluctantly nodded; it was a good beer.

"Proceeds benefit the Native Americans," I said.

Cole opened his mouth to say something but was cut off by a loud noise from the GO© corner.

"Victory!" Ward called, holding up the Connect Four.

"I don't know what hurts worse," Cole said. "Watching this deforestation of a city, or you eloping with the people responsible."

"I mean, if you spent time with them, went into it a bit more objectively, they would cease to be cartoon characters to you," I said.

"Look at your friend's T-shirt, man," he said.

"Yeah," I sighed. Ward did himself no favors, ever. But he was who he was, something I knew Cole respected, somewhere in him, though he wouldn't admit it.

Cole finished his beer.

"There was a time we would've agreed that shirt was irredeemable," he said.

"People grow," I said.

"No, they don't."

I nodded at the bartender, confirming yes, Cole would have another. In my periphery, Kevin and Ward were showing interest in coming over. I held my hand up to them to stay put.

"Wise," Cole said. "Keep those Chihuahuas away from me."

It felt like this was a Cole who would be getting angrier, not more sentimental, the deeper he got into the beers. Mystically, he held his glass up. What we were cheersing, he didn't say. But there was an eeriness to it I didn't like. His beer vanished. He stood from the stool, looking down at me.

"I can't stand this fucking place a second longer."

"All right," I said.

"I just came to say, you don't do what you did via text. Get on your feet."

Even standing, he was still a few inches taller than me. Our faces were close enough that I felt his nose breaths, like a bull. To anyone watching from the GO© corner, this looked like it could turn violent. I worried about Cole doing anything that could leave an impression on GO© upper management when deciding who to take on as a full-time employee.

"Now what?" I said.

"Say it. Say what you said in your text."

"I'm moving out of our place and in with Kevin and Ward."

He gave a smile that made dark spots under his eyes and sent chills through me.

"See you around," he said and walked away.

# COLE

## (38)

I LAY IN bed in the twilight of a bong rip, my iPad propped up on my chest. YouTube's suggestions: scenes from *The Departed*, Kid Cudi music videos, old baseball highlights. The sedative of Mariano Rivera cutters, the fairy dust of vintage homers. I watched one after the other until the algorithm showed its twisted mind and my high school recruitment video was coming up next. I'd filmed it with a friend at West Sunset playground, long before I was a prospect, but it ended up making its rounds among the D1 coaching circuit, leading to eventual scholarships. The autoplay feature had the video going before my stoned ass could press Stop.

"I'm Cole Gallegos, class of 2004 RHP out of San Francisco."

The camera clacks, goes blurry, then refocuses. Seared in digital orange font at the bottom is 9/23/2003.

"I'm six foot, three inches, two hundred and five pounds."

Then I blow a lavender bubble, grape Big League Chew.

I had watched this video so many times I could narrate it blind. Like how the third pitch hisses like bacon, the loudest of the video. I always thought that was the pitch responsible for at least five of the full rides I was offered. I knew that after the fifth pitch, a small plane mows the sky, and the pitch after misses high. I spit after the eighth pitch. Then I move on to curves. The first curve, like the rise and fall of an ocean swell, draws an "Atta babe" from my friend catching me. I watched this former self circle the rubber, swipe dirt crumbs with my cleat, repeat the same movement over and over. Lift, drive, explode hips, whip arm, snap wrist, a dazzling monotony. How could I have ever been so acrobatic and empty-headed?

"I'm Cole Gallegos, a senior right-handed pitcher, and yeah. I hope you like what you saw."

Three minutes was done. My scroll finger became rigid. I knew I shouldn't linger on this page, but swirling in me with the genetics to throw a 95 mph fastball were ones inclined to self-inflicted wounds. The comments beneath the video were a wasteland. I'd subjected myself to them on sleepless nights in Fresno, and now I couldn't help but put my hand back in the flames. Nothing good would come from looking through them, and yet, I scrolled to them.

---

> Help, I forgot how to throw a baseball!!!
> What do I do!?
> —April 30, 2007

> Lol I got a single off him in hs hes a lil bitch hes not that good it makes me laugh how this happened to him
> —May 5, 2008

> Would you guys look at my son's recruitment video and tell me what you think? Copy paste the link thx god bless
> —June 16, 2008

> Wow, Fresno State just won the CWS

> without him. Someone might wanna put this dude on suicide watch
> —July 6, 2008
>
> This guy ran away from his problems like a pussy. If that had been me I would've rode it out. He didn't understand his opportunity, there were a lot of people invested in his future, and he made a selfish and childish decision. Nobody has heard from the kid in years now. Serves him right.
>
> The way I figure, leave him wherever he is.
> —Two weeks ago

---

I laughed, more in self-protection than amusement. That most recent comment was so fresh!

What kind of person was still hung up on this? Enough to watch this video and comment years after any of it mattered? This was becoming the norm. Keyboards absolved people of sense or accountability, enabled denials and fantasies to be lived out. It wasn't just greaseballs in their parents' basements who were doing this, but successful people with careers and families. And we were all just letting it happen. Where was the voice of reason to kick this revolution in the nuts? I thought about Dizzy, whose life did not allow her to hide. It gave her scars and made her sport them to the world. My psychological meltdown had been a spectacle, feasted on by the public. It suddenly was unacceptable to me that so many people thrived from their little crevices, behaving in ways they never would face to face.

I left YouTube and went to Followed. Down at the bottom

of the page was Create New Account.

Just like that, a new person could be born. Anyone. First order of business it asked: profile picture. I uploaded Brad Pitt in *Fight Club*, from the part in the movie when they start to sabotage the status quo, bombing Starbucks, pissing in rich people's food. Next I needed a name. That part was easy. This was an homage to a visionary whose ingenuity came and went without the world having a chance to appreciate it. And this was also his resurrection: Veritas Satire V.

I clicked Create.

Now I was wide awake. I had zero friends. Like a virus, if this project was to thrive like I believed it could, it needed humans. I began with Isaac, clicked Add Friend. I searched names of classmates from college, hitting Request on every one.

My phone buzzed, a text from Isaac. For years, I was used to him being across the hall from me, so close we could hear the other's computer chair creak across the floor, the dresser drawers slide open and shut, the cozy silences of knowing the other was there. But he was across the city with new friends in some neighborhood with hills and dog parks.

> Lol, you Veritas Satire V?

After our falling out at the brewery, he was probably feeling indebted to me, and I saw a chance to take advantage.

> Yeah. Click accept

I texted back. Like that, I had one friend.

I dispatched hundreds more requests. All the nineties names, the Zacks and Brandons, Ashleys and Brittanys. It occurred to me that people might not accept a request from a stranger, which would keep this experiment grounded on the tarmac. But I reassured myself that the flattery of a request, the potential of an extra like, was too much for most people to turn down. Like water, vanity always found a way.

I woke up the next morning, and Veritas had 93 friends. This became 823 friends in one week.

None of whom had any idea who Veritas was. Yet.

**DECEMBER 2010:
EASTERN PROMISES**

## (39)

THIS GIRL, HALEY Denterlein, sat next to me one semester in summer school. I don't believe we ever had a conversation.

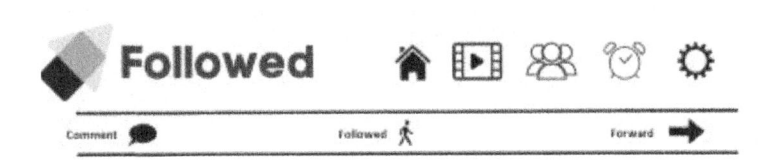

---

**Followed**  🏠 ▶️ 👥 ⏰ ⚙️

Comment 💬   Followed 🚶   Forward ➡️

---

**Haley Denterlein**
Thinking of making some big changes... stay tuned

**Comments:**

> **Josh Warling**
> Ooooh 😊

> **Faith Lovell**
> Conquer the world!

> **Veritas Satire V**
> The suspense! Will she go vegan then quit? Will she start a blog?

# TELL US WHEN TO GO

This dude I met once at a bonfire, and then again on a bus after the Giants game, went to one of the super-private schools that had like two hundred kids.

---

**Bailey Geshner**

My team just wrapped up an intensive quarter on worklife enhancement. Words can't express how proud I am that Salesforce will soon provide its first Ohana room, where there will be an open desk arrangement, and more options of jerky, including tofu and Sriracha Soy. I hope these changes make ripples across the industry, and begin important conversations about human rights in the workplace!

**Comments:**

> **Gary Drapner**
> Mmmmmm Sriracha!
>
> **Locke Voight**
> My company just did a snack data assessment too. Can't tell you what it's done for morale.
>
> **Veritas Satire V**
> Wow, step aside Gandhi. I sure hope you continue to make six figures for this humanitarian work!

Noah Tinden was two grades below me in high school, played JV baseball. He was this aspiring hip-hop academic/class clown type, would go up to crowds at lunch uninvited and freestyle.

---

**Noah Tinden**

Yo yo Just posted my spoof rap video called "Ross Boss." It's about Ross, the department store. Go like it share it, and follow my artist page @TheRapScallion. It's all love. Just a young kid from the city spittin' that truth and knowledge 😊
https://www.followed.com/watch?v=e6QcEChH7eo

**Comments:**
    **Todd Potter**
    Hahaahahahahahaha

**Jessica Van Fleet**
Where do you think of this stuff?

**Veritas Satire V**
Spitting some truth and knowledge: this is bad.

---

Mira Dennison was in my business writing class freshman year at Fresno; we were in a group presentation together. She transferred after that year.

---

**Mira Dennison**

I found an old photo of my dad. Look how much hair he has! Look at those shoes! I was going to save this photo for my Father's Day post, but then I realized, why am I thinking so much in terms of Followed? We need to be present! We should honor our parents EVERY SINGLE DAY! Not just one day a year.

**Comments:**

> **Britt Murphy**
> Amen!
>
> **Madrigal Fairway**
> Just had dinner with mine! They're so awwwwkwarrrddd.
>
> **Stanley Blevins**
> I think about mine every day. RIP.
>
> **Veritas Satire V**
> Maybe you should hang out with your parents with the time it takes you to tell others they need to hang out with their parents.

---

Doris McKray was a Fresno State fan. During my pitching struggles, she waited for me one night outside the clubhouse and in a disappointed tone told me, "You can still be saved," and handed me a Bible.

---

**Doris McKray**

I'M A TUNA SANDWICH. Comforting and trusty! What sandwich are you?
www.followed.com/what-sandwich-are-you

**Comments:**
   **Veritas Satire V**
   Go to bed, Doris.

This was especially exciting for me, to nab Ward into my web. This dude was sharp enough to work for GO©, but not enough to avoid Veritas.

---

**Ward Sullivan**

My dad used to play Emmylou Harris when I was growing up and I would sing along, so he tells me. I've been looking forward to seeing her at the Hardly Strictly BlueGrass festival and reporting back to my old man since I moved to San Francisco just under a year ago. Last weekend I showed up super early to stake out my territory—foldout chair, canopies, snacks, beer—as I was told the place fills up for her. All was going to plan. Then this jackass shows up. First of all, he stood right in front of me and blocked me the whole time, even though I had gotten there first. Second of all, he sang along obscenely loud, and offkey. Like dude, it aint your show.

Respect people's space in a public domain. Respect people's wishes to appreciate art uninhibited. It's really that simple. I thought San Francisco was progressive?

**Comments:**

### John Jacobs
Damn hippies! Lol. Hope you're good bro.

### Alicia Halifax
Ew I hate when that happens. Reminds me of my ultimate pet peeve: when people eat hardboiled eggs on airplanes!

### Josh Nieto
What an idiot.

### Veritas Satire V
You are owed one big apology. Since you've been here a whole 6 months, it is only right that the city make your coziness its top concern. Your opinions on how it should be run deserve deep consideration. That you were unable to eat your Pirate's Booty with a clear view of the stage at a free concert in a public park suggests our city is in great decline. A possible solution: move a few feet to the right, or the left, or better yet, to a completely different city where people won't have the audacity to be near you, living their lives.

---

By this point I was feeling myself a little bit. People who I felt needed a dose of Veritas kept popping into my mind, and each time I hit Comment, a surge of chemicals ran through me. Daryl Seager was a booster and season ticket holder when I was at Fresno. He was my biggest fan during my success, had a cowbell he clanked after strikeouts. It fired me up, I admit, and it was a big part of the personality of my starts. But dude's Followed posts grew hostile during my demise. He posted about how it was time to cut me, how I was jeopardizing lifelong fans. Shit like that. It made me wonder, didn't he know we were Followed friends, that I could see everything he was saying?

Anyway, I went to his page, scrolled through years of his Fresno State sports and Obamacare-is-a-sham posts, all the way back to 2007. One thing I kind of liked about Followed was that it eliminated time. It was the fourth dimension. There could be posts from ages ago, and here I was about to engage with them like they'd just happened. The person might not even feel that way anymore, he might not even remember having felt that way or said that thing, but it didn't matter. Because there it was, waiting for Veritas.

# Followed

Comment  •  Followed  •  Forward

**Daryl Seager**

THIS IS OVERDUE! IS THIS ONE LONG APRIL FOOL'S JOKE? I'm blowing a precious penny on season tickets, for what? It's like I'm watching a fixed game. Is Coach Lonnie caught up with the mob and I don't know? Ha! When are we gonna send Cole packing and get back to Bulldog ball! I don't think he even cares! He must not, to be that bad!!

**Comments:**

### Veritas Satire V

Regarding the Ho Ho's and Marlboro's that you've had to ration to afford season tickets, I speak for everyone: this is tragic. When student athletes of Fresno State don't perform at your standard, something must be done about it! Maybe scholarship money should be taken from underperforming players. Better yet: anytime a player struggles, we hook them to a lie detector and ask them DO YOU CARE? Any irregular results would mean the athlete's scholarship is revoked, and the money is added to your welfare check, plus a can of pork and beans.

I rushed to the bathroom and vomited. This left me feeling light and sharp. There was a liberty to blowing chunks loudly without Isaac coming from down the hall and knocking and saying, "You good?" But also, it felt lonely.

I fell into a heavy sleep. I awoke the next morning to an array of responses. One person commented, "Who the fuck are you?" I promptly responded, "The best friend you didn't know you needed." Some people simply blocked Veritas. But Veritas had also begun to receive likes. I wondered if this was the mindlessness of people liking everything, or if this was evidence of a silenced people seeing a voice represent them. There was even a reply to one of Veritas's comments: "When you're right, you're right." I daydreamt of exploding to anonymous notoriety, getting press, an article on Buzzfeed or Clickhole with a headline like: "Someone is trying to save humanity, one Followed post at a time, but you'll never guess how!"

I liked looking at Veritas's profile pic, Tyler Durden in a tank top and feathered coat with a number-3 buzz cut. Durden—so devilish, so schemey. I felt when I looked at that photo that we were a team, conspiring for good by means of chaos.

Isaac and I had been texting each other zero. I'm sure this was how he preferred it. The thought of me, and his responsibility for our rusted friendship, he probably wanted to avoid. He had been coming home to change after I left for work each morning so we didn't see each other. I could tell from the mess of Modest Mouse and Death Cab for Cutie shirts on his floor. Some nights I found myself standing in Isaac's doorway, staring into his personless room. Isaac kept his door unlocked, and I found it to be an unspoken gesture; the openness of his room to walk in, even snoop if I desired, left open the door of our friendship. Had Isaac decided to lock his room, that would probably be the end of us. It would be Isaac's message that I'd gone from his only friend in the world to someone he didn't want near his belongings.

I had not thought much about what I would do when Isaac moved out. I'd yet to wonder if I'd driven him out, or if the nature of our jobs made us fundamentally different from one another now. Or, was it that we'd really never had anything in common, became friends out of randomness like children on the playground, and we'd finally grown up and realized it?

One night, my phone buzzed, a text from him:

> Dude, I been seeing some of your posts.
> Funny, but also, you ok? You wanna talk about some stuff?

This fucking guy. I shot this reply back at him quickly, not so much to convince him, but to make him think I found him unworthy of a deeply thought-out response.

> Nah man. Haven't felt this good in a while.

I asked: Am I lying to myself? And no, I didn't believe I was. I felt good in my soul, which I hadn't felt since the peak of my baseball years. Which then gave me an idea. I went back to Daryl Seager's page, who, being dumb and old, probably hadn't figured out how to block Veritas from harassing him. I scrolled through the man's gutter of ruminations to another post from 2007, after my downfall.

## Followed

Comment 💬    Followed 🚶    Forward ➡

**Daryl Seager**

Just watched the MLB Draft. Couldn't help but think about Cole Gallegos. Has anyone seen him, at least? He's just a Kid y'all.

**Comments:**

> **Jayce Limerick**
> He sat in front of me in Macro Policy. He just stopped showing up one day mid-semester.

> **Greg Calderon**
> Shows him right. What happens when u run frm ur problems.

> **Liz Bunting**
> Greg is right. If he was my son... I would be Ashamed!!!

> **Veritas Satire V**
> He's found his happy place

## (40)

MR. ANTONINI AND I left school together after the bell. Rain was on the way, you could smell. We grabbed stools at a bar Mr. Antonini chose, facing out at the waning day. The sun was making its way past the Golden Gate Bridge, behind whale-colored clouds. People had their headlights on, and Union Street was congested with Christmas shoppers. It would be dark soon. December in San Francisco was forgettable. Technically we were doing a midyear check-in, but nothing about it felt formal. It was more like Mr. Antonini wanted a drink.

"It's sounding like Delfino will be moving to Contra Costa County after this semester. He has an aunt out there, in a more stable neighborhood, more affordable."

"Will he graduate then?" I asked.

"He'll get his GED, I feel good about that. His aunt is together. Won't let him fuck off. I don't like that Contra Costa gets to have him though, that this city is in essence spitting him out."

Mr. Antonini took a shot like it was something he did, which you would never think with his fleece zip-ups.

"O'Shea has a little more footing, both parents and grandparents in the city. Handsome and talented. His barber swag, talk of getting into music production. Everyone wants to make beats these days. Maybe he's got the ear for it. You an East Coast or West Coast guy?" he asked.

"Like where I'm from?"

"No, beats. Producers. Dre or Dilla?"

"Oh. Both?"

"I love Tupac in an East Coast collab."

"How come you don't play that in 10-B?"

"I'm sure they think Tupac's a dweeb."

He shook his head at the possibility.

More men were accumulating around the bar. They had napkins wrapped around their beer bottles and a sort of practiced way of sipping, then pulling out their phones and blinking impatiently. I couldn't tell if this was a San Francisco that had always been here or if things were mutating this fast.

"Grayson is going to finish up this year here and graduate, then he's off to Fairfield for good. Safeway has a work program with special needs kids, and he's already linked up with a store out there. Majique is back to Modesto, I'm told. Never got her traction here, didn't vibe with her grandma. Got a summer job at the water park, plus more friends back home."

"And then there's Dizzy," I said.

"That's right."

"Cheers," he said and held up his pint glass. "She's still here. I have to believe you've got a hand in that."

I clinked my glass with his.

"To sending her off with a diploma," he said. "We need one more semester from you."

"To Dizzy," I said.

The windows glittered with rain. The bar sounded more like a bar, the jukebox having moved on from the sad ballads of afternoon bar-goers to MGMT. People were dancing and shouting. The energy was like night one on a cruise ship.

"I gotta piss," Mr. Antonini said, then dismounted the stool like it was an unpredictable horse. I started a tab while Mr. Antonini was gone, got us the shot-and-beer deal, a Pabst 16 ounce and Jim Beam. Mr. Antonini didn't wince at it looming there when he returned. It made me feel sentimental for him. I wondered how often Mr. Antonini felt appreciated as a teacher. I played with the words in my mind—I appreciate you—then washed them down with whiskey that bled into my stomach.

\*

The next afternoon the baseball field was thick with the smell of gardenias. Dizzy had a Juicy Juice box without a straw that she squeezed its airy end into her mouth. Overhead was a flock of geese in V formation.

"Aye," Dizzy said, breaking a silence. "Do I stink?"

She tilted her head at the grass and fussed with her hair.

"What?

"You know what I mean."

"Everyone your age stinks. People's bodies are changing. You don't even wanna walk into a boys locker room."

"This ain't no Bill Nye. I'm saying, do I got that smell?"

"What smell?"

She huffed, sped up her voice.

"I go up to my clothes and put my face in it. I don't smell nothing. But Miss Genevieve asked me if we got a washing machine at my house. I'm like, 'Yeah, I do.'"

The geese were gone except for their faint honks.

"So what's my smell?"

Dizzy fitted her baseball glove over her hand and pounded the palm.

"Dizzy," I said and felt overcome by something, a gag reflex of sadness. I tried to erase my tone by quickly throwing the ball. "Fuck Miss Genevieve."

She rolled her eyes and threw it back.

"You gotta know it's not stuck with you. The smell. You can smell like whatever you want. Grass, salt water, new car."

"I want to smell like her," she said. "She smell like people supposed to smell."

She lunged at a bobbing sparrow. It zipped off.

"Birds irritate me."

She unzipped her black coat and pinched it off from the wrist. She flung it, and it ballooned with air and slowly fell. She took her glove off and did arm circles. There was nothing like the first throws after liberating your arm from a jacket. It was like driving with the emergency brake on, then suddenly letting it off. She looked at the ball, twirled it, and poured a heater at my chest. I watched her walk toward the stands of the baseball field, where the usual homeless man lay. She climbed the steps and approached him.

"Hey," I heard her say.

The man stirred.

"This yours now."

She put the jacket across his body, then came back to the field. Dizzy did not seem to want to speak anymore about it. Heading back to campus, we passed the corner store that we'd shopped at prior to her fight. The doors were chained shut, the windows boarded. A sign outside read "Coming Soon: Becky's Vegan Empanadas!"

"Jesus," I said.

"Aye, that's what he get for charging me 15 bucks for some Mambas!"

"Becky's about to charge more."

I pulled up my phone, checked on any activity with Veritas, and I must've smiled at what I saw because Dizzy went, "What?" Such unfiltered fun this venture had been so far. Nowhere in my soul was remorse for how I'd been conducting myself. Just anticipation for more. And it occurred to me, Dizzy too had her grudges, her justified vendettas against the world, and Veritas could be an alleviant for her just as it had for me. She, after all, was a founding father.

"What?" she said again.

I handed my phone to her, watched her scroll.

"Pshhhh," she said after a moment. "You...wow. How long you been at this?"

"Week-ish."

"How you already got eight hundred friends?"

"People are sad."

"*You* sad."

She narrowed her eyes pensively.

"It's given me a new lease on life," I said.

"You about to fuck around and make me concerned."

"Go ahead," I said. "Have a go. You won't regret it."

And so Dizzy began.

## (41)

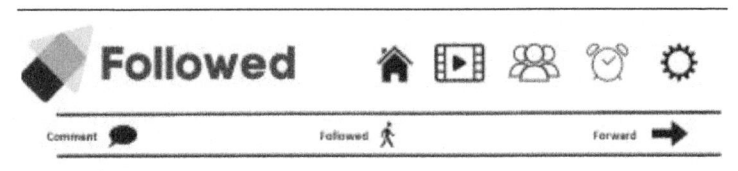

**Followed**  🏠 ▶️ 👥 ⏰ ⚙️

Comment 💬     Followed 🚶     Forward ➡️

**Gregory Shields**
www.followed.com/audio/train-soul-sister
I can't stop listening to Soul Sister by Train! It's so catchy and gives me motivation in the morning! It's my theme song!

**Comments:**

   **Brad Geary**
   I gotta admit, it's catchy.

   **Joshua Peterson**
   Took my kid to the jumpy house yesterday and this song was playing. All The kids were jumping for the moon!

   **Alejandra Rosas**
   This is the song the world needs!

   **Veritas Satire V**
   IF YOU A MAN AND YOU LIKE THIS SONG YOUR WIFE CHEATING ON YOU RIGHT NOW END OF DISCUSSION

**Kathy Yates**

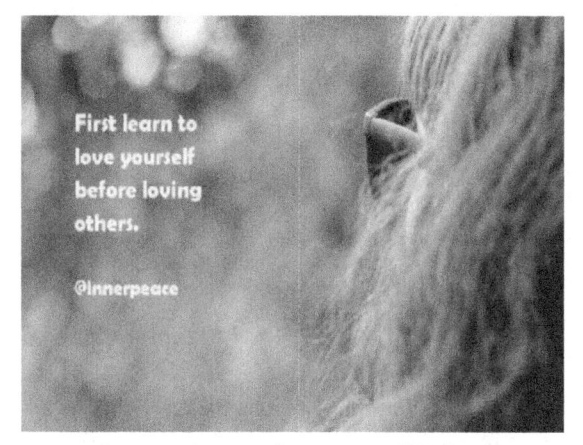

> First learn to love yourself before loving others.
>
> @Innerpeace

Remember, you have to love yourself before you can love someone else!

**Comments:**

### Lacey Madison

more accurate - you can only love another as deeply as you love yourself. And others can show you how much deeper you can love yourself. And it happens both ways at the same time because we all love different aspects of self.

### Drake Lascara

i would disagree. It may be that my experience is different as i had a very caring mother who died when i was 9. After she died i completely shut off the need for connecting with others, and only lived for books, and motorcycles. It was my first relationship at the age of 19 that started me on the journey to loving myself again, and i would still say i love others more than myself.

**Rishyarda LaBonnette**
books and motorcycles? You are my kind of man! You will probably dig my memoir, Moving between the Margins. Motorcycles and books and searching for love and mother all big themes.

**Drake Lascara**
i might check it out sometime. i make no promises as reading for me is an escape from this world, and i often stay away from non fiction as it isn't really escaping our world

**Rishyarda LaBonnette**
I like to think that my memoir offers people a path toward embracing this world.

**Veritas Satire V**
SOMEBODY PACK YALL IN A SPACESHIP AND HIT BLAST OFF SO YALL ALL CAN ESCAPE THIS WORLD!

**Gregg O'Malley**

Here's my violin dubstep album. I been pouring my heart and soul into it, and I decided to release it for free because dubstep is for the people! www.followed.com./audio/5$#55^89*&
Chaos Dat Shit UP by Gregg Da Hazard

**Comments:**

> **Mario Laureano**
> This goes hard bro
>
> **Brittany Avery**
> This is interesting!
>
> **George Colon**
> Keep grindin my dude!
>
> **Veritas Satire V**
> YOU MADE THIS ALBUM FREE BECAUSE AINT NOBODY PAYIN FOR VIOLIN DUBSTEP!

**Jordan Bessler**

Today is World Human Rights Day. What did YOU do?

**Comments:**

    **Laura Siegler**
    So important to be aware. Everyone has rights!

    **Brenda Maffei**
    We are blessed and fortunate and we need to give back any way we can!

    **Jacob Weiss**
    Obama for the win!

    **Veritas Satire V**
    THE FUCK YOU DO JORDAN? SIT ON THE TOILET AND CLICK ARTICLES

THE NEXT DAY at the park, the homeless man was wearing Dizzy's jacket. He waved as we entered. When we were done throwing, I gave Dizzy my phone with Veritas Satire V pulled up. I had admired her work yesterday, and this work was important to continue.

**Paige Driscoll**

I'm so ghetto! 😊

**Comments:**

    **Barbara Finnerty**
    OMG obnoxious

    **Jake Lima**
    Good as new! LOL!

    **Alondra Mensey**
    I did this in college. So embarrassed.

    **Veritas Satire V**
    BITCH BRING YO POTATO FACE TO THE ACTUAL GHETTO AND SEE WHAT HAPPEN

**Clarissa Hawking**

Having workout withdrawals, so I decided to do body squats in my office!

**Comments:**

> **Heather Collinsworth**
> I need to do this!
>
> **Blake Ethridge**
> "I really regret that workout,"—said NO ONE ever!
>
> **Elly Blackwood**
> You're a beast! Grind time!
>
> **Veritas Satire V**
> YOU REALLY JUST DID A PHOTOSHOOT W/ YO PANCAKE ASS.

## (42)

I LAY ON my back, watching clouds slide. My neck tickled from the grass. Not holding my phone made me vaguely tense, like I had a condition and had gone too long without the medication. Dizzy had been quiet for a while, hunched over my phone doing her thing. She chuckled on occasion. These people's lives fascinated her. She read an article someone posted on the Oscar Grant trial and another on how public school salaries no longer supported a family in San Francisco.

"That's how come teachers be leaving all the time. That plus they just weirdoes," she said.

Together we read a piece on how Twitter was growing; in the last year, tweets per day had risen from 10 million to 50 million. Probably, I thought, because it forced people to be brief with their lunacy. Dizzy and I slogged through articles on the recession, trying to understand what exactly it was, why it happened, and how it affected us without our knowing it.

"I think I get it. Like, I was at a barbeque once out in Hayward. It was this OG there who sold hot dogs at A's games talkin' about he just bought a house. He was gettin' hella drunk celebratin', and everybody was all happy for him, but I was just sittin' there like, how you just bought a house from sellin' hot dogs?"

Her nose freckles bunched.

"That's the recession, right?" she asked.

"I guess?"

We were understanding this stupid world on our terms. What was this feeling, I wondered? Like there was nothing there but nothing missing and nothing I would change.

## (43)

I WAS SELDOM called to the principal's office as a kid. But a few times my antics carried me past the teacher's threshold, and I was summoned. Walking to the principal's office, the hallway always felt like a long cavern, my footfalls the only noise. I would walk slowly, considering alternate routes that might take longer. I would think about locking myself in a toilet stall until the end of school to avoid the petrifying ordeal. And now on a Monday morning in December, at age twenty-five, I fidgeted with the tangled class phone cord in 10-B as Mrs. Melvin's assistant asked me to come to the principal's office.

"Like, she wants to see me right now?" I asked. "Sure, no problem."

I hung up and stood by the wall, looking around the class, that old sense of dread coming back. Mr. Antonini was at the board, writing Spanish words with a squeaky marker.

O'Shea had one earbud in and school breakfast on top of his binder. His shoulders were small in his Nautica puffcoat. They would get wider. He would grow into himself, find something to pour his cleverness into, like Mr. Antonini said. Behind him was Delfino. Soon to leave San Francisco for something stable. I hoped his silence didn't undercut him, lead him astray. Grayson was sitting, blinking at the board, copying Mr. Antonini's words like always. His lips shaped the syllables to himself. Someday I might walk into a Safeway and find Grayson there and ask him: Remember our semester in 10-B?

Majique held out her bag of Sour Patch Kids for Dizzy. Always giving. They laughed at something, and Dizzy palmed the desk.

"Dizzy, a ti te gusta los French fries por almuerzo?" Mr.

Antonini asked her.

"Stop playin'," she said. She looked at me and put up her hands. "*What?*"

"*What?*" I parroted.

I smiled. She smiled, and I walked out of 10-B.

## (44)

SITTING IN MRS. Melvin's office was a man I'd never seen.

"This is Dell Chacon," Mrs. Melvin said when I was seated. "He's from the district."

Dell wore a burgundy sweater and had green eyes and a sort of Mr. Rogers disposition. He raised his hand, which was meant to be a wave, but looked more like taking an oath.

"This is all new territory for me," Mrs. Melvin confessed, then sighed. She had a different posture, making her at least a full inch taller. There was also a difference in her tone, meticulous and flat, like an SAT proctor. I could tell this was a persona she preferred not to embody. It made the room feel stuffy, and I thought of the court scenes in TV dramas when a lawyer dabs his temples with a kerchief, pours a glass of water, and takes a gulp before proceeding.

"The tech era is upon us, isn't it?" Mrs. Melvin said. "I'd always hoped to retire before this. I still put email addresses in a phone book."

She was a good principal, didn't talk to people like she had a product to sell. She said what she felt, not what she thought was obligated. She prioritized all kids, not just the ones who made her look good. Which sometimes made the school look bad. She gave second chances, even when parents wanted kids who'd been given nothing in their lives to be expelled and have one less thing. She did her best to feel the gravity of imbalance in San Francisco and the ripple effect on its youth, particularly in public schools.

"Yesterday afternoon Genevieve came to see me, stating she had been attacked."

"Attacked?" I asked. "By who?"

"Well. I'm not sure. The Internet."

I pinched the bottom of my T-shirt and coiled the fabric in my fingers like sod. "Genevieve has an idea who it was. We're just looking for more information."

"Cole," Dell Chacon said and leaned over to squint into Mrs. Melvin's computer. "I wonder if you can have a look. Let's see—" He tapped at the keyboard. "Yes, can you look at this page, the parts that I've highlighted?"

He turned the monitor to face me. "We're looking at the highlighted section."

He then pointed to the highlighted part. I was convinced some people got into law so they could talk to people like they were idiots and not get punched.

"I need to remind you here that I'll be taking notes, and this is on the record," Dell continued, "because we're dealing with district employees and acts of assault that may have been committed during school hours."

A weakness in the bowels fluttered through me like a jellyfish. Dell turned the monitor to face me, which showed Genevieve's Followed page.

## Followed

Comment — Followed — Forward

**Genevieve Dawson**

I am saddened beyond words. Whoever did this, you didn't just damage my house, you damaged my sense of community and my family's sense of safety. When we moved to Marin, the agent said this was a great neighborhood with "built-in" friends. (You'll soon come to learn why I used quotes.) I was excited to be where my children would have space to run in the backyard without worry of a terrorist attack. (September 11 rocked my hometown in Vermont and I'm still scarred). To wake up this morning and find our house had been egged was devastating. We found cracked, and spoiled egg all over our customized windows. My family now feels unsafe. How can we trust our community? We of course are taking appropriate action with Sausalito Police Department.

**Comments:**

> **Gwenyth LaChamplagne**
> This is terrorism!
>
> **Brian Harris**
> Let us know if we can do anything to help. There is such cretinism in the world.

**Veritas Satire V:**
YOU OUT HERE MELTING DOWN ABOUT EGGS.

---

**Genevieve Dawson**

My husband Shiloh and I have sold our house in Sausalito. We did not know if there would be further eggings. Or worse. I loved the area, but this was not worth a life of worry. We were also disappointed in the lack of urgency from SPD. They told us it would be nothing more than a "wild goose chase"! I thought police took pride in their jobs! We just closed on a new home, and are optimistic!

**Comments:**

> **Gary Pescalusky**
> Plenty of fish (homes) in the sea! Give Shiloh my best!

> **Bonnie Magden**
> Positive thoughts on your new chapter!

> **Veritas Satire V**
> NOW YALL MOVING CUZ YALL FELT THREATENED BY EGGS. YOU A SURVIVOR, YOU A COURAGEOUS WOMAN, YOU AN INSPIRATION TO US YOUTH MISS GENEVIEVE.

"Genevieve thinks it could be one of her students, given the vernacular. Plus the fact that this person called her 'Miss.'"

When we were sitting in the grass at Hennessey Field, taking a break from catch, I had not monitored Dizzy's activity—whose profiles she visited or what she said—for a reason: Veritas Satire V required freedom of thought. Dizzy was bright. Brighter than bright. I trusted her estimation of people. Not to mention, what had she even said to Miss Genevieve that was so bad?

"This is being looked at as assault?" I asked.

"Social media has no doubt broadened what constitutes assault, Cole," Dell professed. "Cyberbullying is legitimate and can have serious and even fatal consequences, we are learning. If one of our teachers believes to have been victimized by her own student, then this is something we want to look into."

"She doesn't even have students, really," I said before I realized how bizarre the affront sounded.

"Genevieve mentioned Dizzy and her extended free time," Mrs. Melvin said. "Something about how, given the time of the comments and that they seemed to sync up with her time with you off campus, it seems logical to look to Dizzy."

"It's not free time," I said. "You know this better than anyone else. You said it yourself that it was recreation for her mental health."

I craved the brisk funk of the pier just down the block from Galileo now more than ever, where the Vietnamese men fished and where Dizzy and I sometimes passed on our walks. I wanted to speculate something silly with Dizzy, such as the phenomenon of a built pier. How did the first man who wished to stand over the water but not fall in make it real? Who decided it was possible to drive a tremendous wooden pole through choppy waters into sand? And then do it dozens of times to get farther out there. And somehow none of it would eventually wash away?

"Can you tell us, has Dizzy been on her phone during your

time off campus?" I sat in a silence that Mrs. Melvin did not push. She went on.

"These have been some very positive months for Dizzy. There has been serenity with her. She seems to have a curiosity, a sincerity to her. You've shown her some adults can be trusted. I've even seen a change in you. Your shoelaces don't drag on the floor. You have a look you didn't have the first day we met, a look like this is a world you might be willing to participate in. So I want to say that if it turns out Dizzy sent the messages to Genevieve, it's not your fault, Cole. You did more than was asked of you."

"They weren't messages," I said.

"I'm sorry?" Dell Chacon said.

In my mind, I was deflecting culpability from Dizzy. Being that the posts were public, I dumbly felt they were less targeted, less assaulting than a personal message. But how it came out was, I knew something about who sent them. Dell took this as an opportunity to lay out some legal terms I didn't listen to.

"Cole," Mrs. Melvin said softly, as though to relieve the room of Dell. "Who is Veritas Satire V?"

# ISAAC

**(45)**

AUDREY APPEARED IN the doorway of the GO©-To Cafe and took a seat across from me.

Something about it felt premeditated, like she'd been looking for me. I told myself to act like I had when we ran into each other in the Marina last month—smooth-ish, but real, vulnerable. Since that night, I'd known we had a connection. Platonic, sexual, or otherwise, I wasn't sure. But it was more than strictly work in our eye contact, our engagement. I knew we had more half-smiles, more caught glances from across the room than others. I told myself, if she's come to offer the interview in person rather than via email like she's done with everyone else, don't flip out.

"How are you holding up?" she asked.

I told her I was enjoying the Denmark project, seeing photos of Copenhagen, the ice-cream-flavor houses on canals as I mapped bike paths.

"Working at GO© is like traveling the world, but in comfort and luxury."

"Isn't it incredible?"

"I'm so comfortable here that sometimes I don't wanna leave."

Waiting for her to respond, I thought maybe this was the time to reveal my brainchild, the emergency call plan. Not the whole thing, just some wafts of it, the concept and inspiration. Something was off though. The way she was looking at me, plain and indiscriminate, like she was artificial intelligence gathering data to report somewhere.

"I've even slept here a handful of nights in the last month," I said.

"Have you?"

"Trying to shrink the queue, keep the projects from stalling."

I thought this was the kind of tidbit she would appreciate and perhaps pass onto upper management: He puts his work first, doesn't fold, has a personality and a pulse.

"How are the accommodations?" she asked. "In the Recharge Room?"

"Five-star."

I had assumed she would grab something from the wall of cold paninis and eat it with me, but she was just sitting still, looking possessed.

"Burnout is fairly common," she said as though we'd been on the topic. Her tone had this phony concern, like something from *Mean Girls*. "There's nothing to be ashamed of."

I wondered if indeed we had been talking about it, though I didn't know it. There was a dreamlike incongruity in our communication. She tapped her hands on the table conclusively.

"Let me know if I can help in any way," she said.

She scooted back and was off. Some percent of me thought maybe this was a prank. Had they been monitoring me and determined a lag? My queue had unresolved issues, sure, but so did everybody's. It was impossible for there not to be. I was putting in fourteen-hour days; I'm sure that showed up in their surveillance. And if they really were keeping close tabs, they'd also probably noticed that I barely ate any of the free food anymore so as not to contribute to overhead. I was an ideal employee. I knew it.

Later that day, Ward had his FTE interview. It wasn't in the maps department but marketing and sales; they "saw something" in him. He was hired directly and told us that the interview "seemed like more of a formality." He was set to begin training next week. They were flying him to Austin. He mentioned we should transfer over there with him: "Mad perks."

After work, the three of us went to the new trampoline place down at Crissy Field. It was a kid spot, a birthday party hotbed, with a private room for pizza and cake. But we'd heard companies like Twitter had hosted company functions there. This tech wave enjoyed embracing activities that past generations would have gracefully let go of by adulthood. Job interviews over ice cream with sprinkles, men with full beards playing Twister.

As we jumped around, Ward, who apparently took gymnastics as a kid, kept saying, "Check this out," then did something like land on his back. He brought up the apartment, the urgency of locking in a lease. I told him pretty plainly that I thought I needed to wait to find out about the GO© interview before I committed. This concern did not compute with him.

"I mean, we still gotta get it, right?" he asked. "Way too much value to leave on the table."

"Yeah," Kevin said. "GO© hasn't given me an interview yet, but I'm still going ahead with the apartment"

"How?" I asked. "What if you don't get the job? I don't get the concept of value if there's no money to afford it."

"I can tell," Ward said, then made this hiccup noise following a somersault. "Let me know ASAP 'cause we got our eye on a three-bedroom. They got an open house next weekend. But if you're out, then we gotta pivot. I'm not getting stuck with some Craigslist hobbit for a roommate."

We went to the dodge ball arena, where there were a bunch of kids fresh from school release, hair matted to their ears. We separated into two teams. Kevin and Ward were on one side. I was on the other with a couple kids and a teenage employee. In the initial mad dash for the dodge balls, Ward shouldered a kid into a padded wall. I got two balls and fell back into safety. My first order of business was to drill Ward straight in his nose. The way he looked all bewildered and checked for blood satisfied me. He gave this childish look like the world wasn't fair and he wanted someone to reimburse him. I threw another one and blew up his ear. He was unaware I'd thrown it.

"I'm out already!" he cried.

When I got to work the next day, I had a few new emails: LinkedIn saying a Blaine Ferguson from Boomerang Solutions had viewed my profile, a company-wide email from GO© with the subject "Welcome Aboard New Executive Associate of Sales Ward Sullivan." Another huge sale was happening at Best Buy. Couched in these emails was something from GO© Team. I was so used to disregarding emails from companies as spam, that I initially glossed over it. The subject was:

---

You're Going To Want To Read This. Yep You:)

---

I didn't click it immediately. I felt like a high school kid with a college admissions letter; once I opened it, whatever it said was decided. It was breathtaking, the unapology of words written and not said, with no eyes or eyebrows or intonation.

---

Dear Isaac,
Over the last quarter, GO© has made great strides. Literally. We've been real trail blazers over here! We think the world is a pretty cool place, and it should be seen in all its glory. You have been integral to our present and our future! We've got more routes to configure beyond driving. We want to help walkers and public transit users find their way. We've got canals and rivers to map.

The future is looking bright here at GO©! Keep on truckin', dude!
Best wishes going forward,
GO© Team

---

People probably thought I was hard at work, the way my face was furrowed at the email. I closed all my other tabs. What the fuck was that? I couldn't ask Ward and Kevin their thoughts for fear of what they'd tell me. Was I capable of going about my work as though I hadn't seen that email? Technically, did I even have work to do anymore? Long had I marveled the communication of the GO© workplace, its empty giddiness, its strategic broadness. It was so effective. I had never been on the receiving end of it until now though. The reality was it sucked.

In the bathroom, I splashed my face, put my hands under the air dryer, and listened to its calm hum. The light was off in Audrey's office when I passed it. I tried to glance inside, for anything, a clue. I wondered if she had cameras that notified her if someone was being lurky. GO© was in the practice of lessening the privacies of the public; who knew what other twisted technologies they'd innovated in that realm as protection for themselves. Maybe weight sensors in the flooring that could identify who was walking where and when, and trapdoors when someone went postal?

Back at my desk, I clicked New Message and typed in Audrey's email:

Subject: RE: YOU'RE GOING TO WANT TO READ THIS. YEP YOU:)

Hey A,
Can you ping me when you get a chance. No biggie, just a quick Q.
Thanks!!
Isaac

---

She pinged me right back, almost before my message sent.

---

Subject: AUTO-REPLY OUT OF OFFICE THRU 12/20

Hello!
I will be out of the office through the week of 12/13 with limited access to internet. I'm in the Yukon, spearheading the next GO© initiative: dogsledding routes. Just kidding! (Or am I?)
See you next week!
Audrey

---

I slid around in my chair side to side. It glided across the short carpet with such ease, it was like Mary Poppins skipped around each night and WD-40'd the wheels.

I logged off my iMac, then closed my MacBook and sat there breathing for a minute. I packed my things into my North Face Borealis; there wasn't much: just my iPod bicep sleeve for when I worked out, a GO© sunscreen stick, 3D glasses for the GO© theatreplex. Those items gone, my desk looked uninhabited, like I'd never been there.

The exit slid open, and I was hit with Mountain View sun reflecting off pavement. I turned back inside, straight to the Odwalla refrigerator. I took one out. Then another, a Mango Tango. Then three more because, fuck it, everyone has their ways of being hurt. I didn't feel bad about taking the balls in college, and I didn't feel bad now. My revenges, comparatively, were minuscule. When I walked away, the fridge was as barren as my desk.

## (46)

LATER THAT AFTERNOON, I found out Kevin got the same cryptic email as me.

"It never actually says we're fired though," I said.

"Yes. It does. This is denial, Isaac," Kevin said. "I don't even know why you're trippin'. Are you not seeing that San Francisco is an oasis for guys like us right now? Capable, educated, intrinsically motivated? You literally have to try to not get a job in this market, especially in tech."

"And especially if you have GO© on your resume," Ward added. "All these startups want dudes with industry experience. Just scrape up the first month's rent. Get your resume updated. Then? Start pinging startups." Ward did the universal jack-off motion. "Simple."

"Yeah. I already have an interview with Quora," Kevin said.

"What's Quora?" I asked

"What's Quora?" Ward butted. "It's this website where you ask obscure questions, like 'I got a letter from Bank of America asking me for my Social Security number. Is it a scam?' and people will, like, answer. There's also Reddit, which is headquartered here too."

"What's Reddit?"

"It's this website where you talk about random shit. Like, 'Did anyone see Lady Gaga's eyebrows at the Grammys?' and people will go back and forth about it. I spend whole bus rides on it. The CEO 'spez' went to UVA. He also just launched Hipmunk, a travel-planning search engine. If Reddit IPO's, I'll hop on them early. There's also Tumblr? You've at least heard of Tumblr, right?"

"Tumblr?"

"Dude, where have you been? It's a blog service, like Followed, where you put pictures of yourself or whatever."

"Like Instagram?" I asked, which I'd only heard of.

"Yeah, but Tumblr is different. Like you can categorize. Oh, and there's Survey Monkey."

I brought my hand to my chin, pretending like I'd heard of them.

"Survey Monkey is this service that allows you to ask questions to people and get their answers."

"So like Quora."

"No. Because it itemizes the data. The point is, dude, you can work in this industry. Investors are funneling capital into these ideas. Somebody is set for life right now because of fuckin' Angry Birds. We all got more to offer the world than that, bro. Imagine how dumb it is that all this money is out there, but it goes to someone else."

"It's true," Kevin said. "Don't really see the point in living here unless you're taking full advantage. You're knocking on the door. You have the resume and the look for one-percent-level income, man. At least five percent."

I felt like I was in some intense movie scene where someone says, with guns pointed every which way, "You're either with us or against us." The longer I said essentially, "I can't afford that lifestyle with no job," and they replied essentially, "See, you're just not getting it," the easier my decision became. I told them I'd let them know ASAP, but they knew I was out.

Outside their place, I caught a cab to the Sunset apartment. We passed the KK Café at Haight and Divisadero. It had a sign that read "Since 1965." The different tech bus lines in front of it were so long they suffocated the entrance. I tried to get a glimpse inside. It seemed empty. Possibly out of business.

I cracked my window. The cab caught a few green lights on Fell. We cruised past gas stations, the DMV, the homeless of the panhandle. A feeling surged in me to tell the guy to hang a right on Stanyan and just go—past the Marina, past the city. That was what I wanted. To hop on the Golden Gate Bridge and hug the coast, or maybe cross the Bay Bridge, head through the seedy Mantecas all the way to Yosemite and put my head under a waterfall. Move, move, move.

I scrolled on my iPod. So many soundtracks felt appropriate right now. My shell-shocked state was best encapsulated by Philip Glass's arrangements for *The Hours*, but I didn't want that right now. I slid down to Hans Zimmer, his soundtracks with such majesty like *The Last Samurai* and *Inception*, then back up to my robust Howard Shore catalog, all the adventure and brotherhood of *Lord of the Rings*, the palpating doom of *Seven*—all of these had something I needed or felt connected to at this moment. But there was another song that felt as though it was made for this moment, this sudden taste for unknown land, unknown future.

The grappling with not knowing who you are and wanting a new beginning. I scrolled through my library, and I played *Eastern Promises*.

## (47)

THE CURTAINS WERE shut as usual at our house. Being from the Sunset made Cole some kind of species oblivious to sun, maybe even allergic. He was likely at work, but even the possibility of him had me pacing up and down the block, unable to bring myself to go up the steps. I hadn't seen him since our brewery breakup, which left me scared. I pulled out my phone, a tic. I looked at my last exchange with him, though I knew exactly what it was. I'd looked at it many a night on Ward and Kevin's couch: my text that I was moving out. His zero reply. My question of "Are you OK?" His reply of "Never better." What a fucking cemetery of a chat. I was ashamed.

I finally built the courage to go up the steps, this time carrying a bag of El Burrito Express carne asada burritos with extra green salsa and a melon drink. I knew this was the best way, stronger than words, to express that I had I fucked up. I opened the door, and it was like I'd put my nose in gym shoes. On the TV was an Icy Hot commercial with Shaq. I heard a feeble sigh from the couch. There he was, one shoe on his foot, the blanket covering his waist. His head was bent back over the armrest like some Picasso painting. He moaned, his head rolled. His eyes found me.

"Whoa," he said, then put out his hands as if to defend himself. "What time is it?"

"One," I said.

He sat up. I held out the heavy brown bag. By now, he smelled it. We shared a look, one in which he seemed to be reading me, suspicious that I was there to announce I'd been hired full time so we could celebrate my prosperity. He must've seen my flattened spirit because he accepted the bag, sat up, and brushed the weed debris off the table. The ritualistic procession of a burrito commenced, the reaching in the bag, the unspiraling of the foil. As he chewed the first bite, he nodded, like he'd heard a notion with which he was in agreement. Steam weaved through the top. He uncapped his green salsas, poured both into the open wound of the burrito. He took another circumferential bite. The passion with which he unlidded his melon drink and channeled it was like a nineties Gatorade commercial.

Cole finished his burrito and did not spend a moment to catch his breath, just submerged his forearm into the bag, came up with the second one, which I'd intended to eat, which he probably knew. He also knew I wouldn't stop him. Like our friendship had mastered at this point, we were wordless.

Eventually Cole explained what had happened to him yesterday, how he told the principal that all the Veritas comments had been his. The principal knew Cole was lying, but let him go ahead with it to protect Dizzy. Cole was fired on the spot. When Mr. Antonini found out what happened, he texted Cole to meet him at the bar when he got out of school. There, Mr. Antonini shared that he was moving out of San Francisco at the end of the school year. His landlord was selling the building, and the new buyers said they were renting to a family. All six apartments. It was a loophole landlords had found to beat rent control in San Francisco, the same loophole Kevin and Ward would be leveraging for their apartment in the Marina. The cheapest studios in San Francisco were now 3k a month, which was Mr. Antonini's whole paycheck. So he was looking to head east—Oakland, Berkeley, El Cerrito, Richmond—because if he was getting shoved to the edge of the bay, so were the kids. Or farther; the edges they were being pushed to probably were so distant that there was no bay anymore.

"We drank some fuck-the-world shots," Cole groaned on the couch. "Then some farewell shots. I don't remember what time it was when we left the bar, except I'm pretty sure it was still light. Then the day got interesting."

I assumed this meant he got lost. Or accidentally ordered a $50 truffle sandwich.

"I woke up with that morning-after dread," he said. "I worried Veritas had gone on a rampage, on some *Fight Club* multiple personality shit. But I went through my phone, and miraculously I was too drunk. Though I did manage to text Mr. Antonini a heart emoji and "'sup."

The room was putrid from Cole's steaming pores now that the hot sauce had him sweating.

"But there was something else."

Cole showed me his phone call history, and I saw that he had received a call from our old coach, Lonnie, last night at 7:30.

"You answered?" I asked.

"Apparently. Look, it says we talked for twelve minutes."
"About?"
"I have no idea."
"Dicey territory."
"Then this morning, an email popped up from him. Look."

---

Subject: NICE TO CATCH UP. SOUNDS LIKE YOU'RE DOI...

Nice to catch up. Sounds like you're doing great. And to learn you are working with kids in need. Those kids are lucky. I waited this long to reach out because people need space, and I wanted to respect that. Like I said, the community never stopped asking about you. Or caring. You were tangled up in yourself. You couldn't know your imprint on this town. When we won the College World Series the year after you left, it wasn't no accident. We were a goddamn grease fire. Which you started. I'm so glad to hear you are willing to throw out the first pitch at our alumni game, January 25, 2011, 5:00 p.m. When I called you last night, I thought for sure you'd say no. I needed a beer just to get up the courage to ask. But you didn't even flinch, said yes right away. I was shocked! Let's show you what you meant and continue to mean to the Bulldog community.

Be in touch, M

---

"I've been refreshing my email all morning, hoping it will go away," Cole said.
"Have you been away long enough?" I asked.
"From what? Fresno?"
"Baseball, everything."
"I don't know. No."
"Is this the end of Veritas?" I asked.
"Prolly.

"Do you think Veritas was a net positive or net negative?" I asked.

"Shut up," he said.

He looked up blankly, like he was trying to catch sunlight to sneeze.

"Don't you have work?" he asked.

"About that."

I told him what happened, and he laughed at how hard I'd bought into the culture, just to be cut out with a clown email.

"You shoulda crocheted your boss a scarf," he said.

I didn't vocalize it, but I wished I'd thought of that myself.

"Well, your bed's right where you left it," Cole said. "And there's still a hard-boiled egg in the fridge, which I'm pretty sure is yours 'cause I don't know how to make those. Let's see. Oh, you'll be happy to learn the house still gets thirty below at night."

"What if we don't stay here?" I asked.

"We can't afford to move somewhere else, dude. We don't have jobs."

"No. I mean in this city. What if we don't stay in this city?"

I hoped it came off like an epiphany, but I'd been thinking more and more in the last couple weeks: What was my plan B?

"Toward the end of my time at GO©, I had a weird feeling. Something felt off. Like when you think your girlfriend might be cheating on you."

"You've never had a girlfriend."

"Thank you. Point is, I've been mulling over some contingency plans."

Cole laughed condescendingly, as in, listen to you.

"There's a company called Uber, headquartered in San Francisco."

Cole threw up his hands, already repulsed.

"It's set to be up and running in other major cities in the US over the next year. They have big-time global investors in Europe, Beijing."

"This reeks of Ward."

"He told me about it, yes."

"Can that guy say one thing that doesn't make me wish for human extinction?"

"No. Him and Kevin told me about all the hot startups. Uber is a new cab service that allows you to order rides from people in their regular cars."

"That's a terrible idea!" Cole cried. "If I have the option of a hipster blaring Skrillex in his Prius and a regular yellow cab, I'm going yellow cab. Right? What is happening to people?"

"Uber disrupts the age-old image of someone standing in the rain trying to hail a cab," I said. "You order it to you, and the nearest one comes."

"Disrupts." Cole sighed. "It stopped raining in San Francisco in the nineties."

"What do you want from me?" I asked.

"I don't get it. If you want to work for them and they're in San Francisco, what's this about leaving?"

"I don't want to work in the office. Not for all the Odwalla in the world."

"I'd do anything for an Odwalla."

"Oh!"

I tugged my backpack off the couch, unzipped it, and the bottles somersaulted out, still mildly cold.

"Have your pick."

Cole grabbed a Green Monster.

"I want to be one of the drivers," I continued. "New places. Fresh air. GO© Maps showed me what's out there, but in pixelated cartoons. The Chicago River. The Grand Canyon. Sixth Street, Austin, Bourbon Street, New Orleans. I want to see them for real, everything I can. Everyone's telling me now is the time to nail the money job. But this could be the time to do a lot of things."

"How about meth?"

Cole was algae-lipped from the drink.

"OK. Where do I fit in?" he asked.

"You can drive too. All you gotta be is twenty-one and not a murderer."

"No degree?"

"Not to drive a car, man."

"It pays all right?"

"No."

"I am a connoisseur of such jobs."

"Hear me out. We start in San Francisco. Maybe someone has us drop them off in Napa or down in Monterey. We check that spot out. Decide to stay a night. Then keep cruising north or south. Maybe one night we book it to Vegas. Or we pull an all-nighter to Seattle. Or Salt Lake. Pack the trunk with a small cooker, sleeping bags, spend some nights under the stars. One night, on some long, empty stretch, drive 150 miles per hour. Tailgate a college football game. Buy a cougar a martini at a metropolitan happy hour. See autumn in Boston. We can work as much as we want or as little as we want. Stick in a city until it's time to move on. I can be Kerouac, you can be Moriarty."

"Who?"

"Did you ever not Sparknotes a book in high school?"

"Nah."

Cole blew his nose into a brown napkin, then leaned back into the couch.

"I don't need to be in this city right now," he said. "Getting hella weird."

He shook his head at a thought, reached into the small plastic container, and fished out a pickled jalapeno.

"What about a car?" he asked.

"I saved enough to buy one."

"Must be nice. How much do you have?"

"Enough."

"How much?"

"Enough, why?"

"If we do this, I need a favor," Cole said.

"How much?"

"Enough."

He sucked in air to cool his tongue.

"Ideally, I'd pay you back someday. Ideally."

# COLE

**(48)**

DIZZY ONCE TOLD me that traveling the Bay Bridge eastbound was like entering the mouth of a whale.

"One of them whales that be drifting wit its mouth open, like ahhhhh."

Now that I was on the Bay Bridge, I wished to be back on the grass of Hennessy Park, playing catch, telling her, "Yeah, that's exactly what it's like." Especially at 6:45 a.m. in December, with the sun just starting to make hushed purples in the dark. The initial bottleneck of the bridge had loosened, and now cars were traveling freely, deeper into the whale.

Isaac switched to the leftmost lane. My window was down, the exposed part of my neck chapped by the air. Isaac took the exit onto the island, and we were soon moving slowly along the water, our tires popping on loose gravel. We approached a white Ford Windstar with its trunk open. A tall man with a square tuft of hair on the back of his head juggled fishing rods and a tackle box down the jetty. His boxers puffed out of his sagged jeans like a chef's hat. Then the man was in our rear view, crouching down onto the rocks beside someone who was already seated, his line in the water.

We pulled up to a stop sign. Three generations of women waited to cross in the morning dark. The grandmother wore a gold hijab and used a cane. With her other hand she held the granddaughter's hand; the girl wore a shimmering turquoise hijab and carried a boxy pink backpack. The mother walked beside them, holding her daughter's lunchbox, talking on the phone.

"This is Sturgeon Street," Isaac said, leaning his head out to view the street sign.

"Keep going," I said.

We passed a park. A cluster of kids, middle school age, was on the swings in some playful debate.

Their sounds disappeared behind us as we passed Striped Bass Street, where there was a washing machine on a front lawn. Down the block was a vacant lot, a sign posted: NO ALCOHOL, NO TOBACCO.

"Park," I said. "We're a little early."

I got out, and geese honked wearily somewhere in the fog. I squinted and made out an infield and pitcher's mound. There were bleachers and a little press box. This was a baseball field for kids not much bigger than the geese currently occupying it. I found myself touched by the press box, its toylike proportions. Dizzy had mentioned this field before, and when she had, I had quietly determined she was lying, that there was no way there would ever be a ball field on Treasure Island.

The sky was getting bluish. Out past centerfield, were shipping containers, idle and rusted. Beyond leftfield was a dense pile of cinder block, a chalky haze of permanently unsettled dust above it. The Oakland cranes loomed in the distance like futuristic surveillance.

"It's time," I said to Isaac, who sat in the idling car. "Wanna come watch?"

"This is your thing," he said. "I'll stick behind."

I joined a small crowd moving toward Striped Bass Street. Black women with long, artful nails and old Asian men in masks walked together toward the bus stop. There were college-age kids with withdrawn faces, off to class or jobs. Grandparents called to grandchildren in Spanish, Arabic, English, offering parting messages for the day. MUNI buses squelched.

1403 Flounder Street was a mushroom-colored house

crowned with a satellite dish. It had a screened-in porch with shoes scattered at the top step. A tricycle was half-sunk into the patchy grass of the front yard. I was positioned behind a holly bush, waiting, starting to feel regretful of this plan, just like the night at the abandoned hospital.

Then, creeping down Flounder with tinted windows was a black Town Car. Its slowness gave off the vibe of a hit man. When it stopped in front of 1403, a tall man in a tattered dress coat stepped out. He took off his chauffeur's hat and gave his eyes a morning rub.

The screen door at 1403 neighed. The girl there pulled a sweater off a clothes hanger outside where it had been hanging. She put it up to her nose and smelled, then started to fuss one arm through. When her sweater was on, she untangled her earbuds, put them in, and raised her eyes to the day for the first time.

"Miss?" the man asked. She stopped abruptly.

The black car gave her alarm, I could tell, as though it might be a branch of authority she didn't know was after her.

"Miss?"

She squinted, made out the man's raggedy state, and slackened her shoulders. "Bruh, you lost. Ain't no Princess Diana here."

The driver looked back in his car as though there must be a mistake.

"Hold up the damn sign," I whispered to myself, a feature I'd splurged the extra $45 for, being that it was Isaac's money.

"Dizzy Benson?" the man asked. "To Seaside High School?"

He held up a laminated paper: Elite Limousines, Dizzy Benson. Then he walked to the back door and opened it. Dizzy let out a "Ha!"

"Corny ass!" she yelled, as though she sensed I was somewhere near. By now the sun was reaching over the flats. I watched it hit her reluctant smile, which I had seen on mornings in 10-B when she came in lit off Mambas, looking like she could either hug Grayson or rip a motivational poster off the wall. She peered inside the car.

"The fuck you doin' with the *Dumb & Dumber* car?" a girl called at her.

"Whatchoo mean? This my car. Pass me the Grey Poupon, skank!"

The man closed the door behind her. Immediately her window slid down, and her face appeared, her hair flipping out into the day like tinsel.

"See y'all musty asses at school!"

The Town Car turned off Flounder and joined the crawl of cars toward the Bay Bridge.

"Hey, Ivan, suck it!"

The jetty-studded shore, white-capped from bird shit, was like a postcard of the Himalayas. I closed my eyes. The air was still enough that I could hear the bay licking up against the rocks. I imagined that when the car curved onto the bridge, Dizzy would scoot from side to side, looking out both windows at the city, at things she'd never seen on MUNI through the crowd and crossing bars, thinking something like: So this my city.

The Town Car moved slowly and was easy to follow at first. Advancing toward the west entrance, it resembled a rollercoaster in its rickety ascent until it became a black freckle on the island. Before I turned to head back to Isaac, a sound pierced the lull.

"Corny ass!"

## JANUARY 2011:
## TELL ME WHEN TO GO

## (49)

I'M ON THE top step of the dugout, where I used to stand before my name was announced.

There're whiffs of tailgate barbecue, and dusk makes the outfield glow peach. It's dreamlike, how beautiful this game is. I sense a heaviness, a suction on my left hand. My glove. A hand comes down gently on my shoulder. I follow it up the arm to Coach Lonnie, standing beside me. I look up into the stands, where everyone is on their feet. I let my eyes adjust, waiting to discover a dead relative waving or something else impossible. But I don't. Because this is not a dream, like the dozens I've had leading up to today, all of which left me dry-mouthed, clutching my chest in bed. Today it's real. Lonnie pats my shoulder.

"Go listen," he says close enough to my ear that I can hear his old rattle. As I move onto the field, the crowd cheers, a shape-shifting blob of sound.

Here I am, on the mound. In Converse Chucks, I don't feel the crunch, the satisfaction of spikes sinking into dirt. I feel granules against the soles of my feet. This is just like a scene out of *The Sandlot*, the way the game should be. It should be a field of weeds and kids. No boos. No coaches charting every goddamn thing with their stern faces and side comments. No scouts with their scout speak, breaking people down to data.

"He is in the top five in every pitching category in Fresno State history," the PA announces. "He was in our hearts in 2008 on our glorious Cinderella run."

The crowd whistles. Someone yells at the top of his lungs, something I don't make out.

"He is a beloved member of the Bulldog community, here

to throw out the ceremonial first pitch for tonight's alumni game. Let's give a warm applause, and a big welcome back, to one of our favorite alumni, Cole Gallegos."

"Tell Me When To Go," by E-40, my old walkout song, begins to play in the stadium.

The whole crowd used to thizz dance as I threw my warm-ups, waves of motion, people crouching, flossing spicy frowns, pinkies in the air. They were my own army back then. I hear the goofy chorus, "Tell me when to go, Tell me when to go!" And I'm thinking: Now. Right now.

I'm at the base of the mound, because standing right on top of the mound might stir up memories. Plus, that's for the Nolan Ryan types, the ones who want to prove they can still throw gas. Alternately, standing way in front of the mound is for the geriatrics. Somewhere in the middle, that's where I belong now.

The crowd is ongoing static. I feel myself about to consider all the speculation going through the park, all the curiosities of whether I'll flub this pitch, shit the bed for old times' sake. Instead, I close my eyes and put myself in the last place I threw a ball.

The sounds of nearby tennis. The dew in the shadows of the cypresses that bit my ankles. The clips of grass that clumped at my shoes. Dizzy, clumsy with her big glove. Impatient, frowning. Her hair fluffing in its undefinable way. The back-and-forth of catch, all a kind of simple song. When I met Dizzy, my life was verging in different directions, and without having known her, I would never have found it in myself to make it back here—the epicenter of my lowest moments. I was the one who was supposed to give Dizzy guidance; it's funny how that turned out. It occurs to me now that I never got to thank her. For showing me that to be true and honest is precious in this life, no matter how some see it. And, really, I never thanked her for being my friend.

I step long, and the ball glides from my fingertips, headed at my target, who is not Dizzy, but Fresno State's backup catcher. It's a perfect strike, with tilt, snagged right at the knees. The catcher sticks it as though waiting for the umpire's call. The cheers bring me back. Twenty years of baseball memories flood over the dam I built in my mind, all the way back to my first time holding a hardball as a boy, its seams mercilessly firm. I remember the excitement that this game could cause. The camcorders and lawn chairs of weekend tournaments with the snack shacks and bad T-shirts. The period in high school when kids only reached base on dropped third strikes from my sliders. Then the golden years, brief as they were, when standing ovations like this were standard.

"We love you, Cole!"

This is a curtain call for a vanished career. Do I take off my hat and wave how I used to after eight shutout innings? Does this one meaningless pitch merit the same exit as a whole night of flawless pitches? I stop just short of the baseline, still on the infield grass. I put the sleeve of my shirt to my eye. When I take my hand away, everything is blurry. A miniature figure is in front of me: Lonnie, whose chin—with its eternal stubble that made a scratchy noise when he rubbed it during postgame talks—begins to quiver as he pulls me in. We embrace.

"Ain't fair, kid," he says. He tries to say more but shakes his head, knowing it would be blubber.

Isaac waits on the top step of Fresno's dugout. I walk to him, put my head into my friend's collarbone, take in the smell of his laundry, the smell of his room, which conjures memories of talks and movies. It brings a Pavlovian response of sanctuary. I feel Isaac's collarbone against my teeth. I realize I've been screaming and have run out of breath. Isaac claps both his hands on my shoulders, then my cheeks. I shake my tears out, taste my own salt. I keep my head down, for once not to forget, but to remember.

Isaac and I sneak out the back of the clubhouse before the

alumni game begins. In the parking lot, we hear applause as Fresno State takes the field to "Who Let the Dogs Out?"

"That pitch was mighty George Bushian, I gotta hand it to you," Isaac says. "Though I will say, you didn't do it in the face of terrorism and war."

"Noted."

"But given your past, that pitch might've been more of an accomplishment than George's."

"Good to know."

"And, you know, Bush had his whole triumphant strut after. You kinda just melted."

"All right, thanks."

Hours later, we are in the middle of Death Valley. I pull off, piss in the chill of the night. There are no cities, no campfires, just smoky galaxies with blinking stars like buoys in the bay. I am still behind the wheel when the sun peaks into our windshield. We'd planned a stop in Vegas to gamble a few blackjacks and drink a cocktail and chortle at the misery of it all. But it was 4:45 in the morning when we arrived. Isaac was snoring, and I was so dazed in thought I barely noticed the neon of the city passing, one casino at a time. I was thinking about how easy that pitch had been. I dotted the glove. I couldn't help but wonder, were my yips gone? In all my days of catch with Dizzy, not one slipped toss. That was months of controlling the baseball. All I would need to do was call a scout—I still had some of their texts in the recesses of my phone. I could throw a few innings, take a minor league contract. A Hollywood story. Organizations loved those; they sold tickets. But maybe that was greedy. Delusional, like all the Vegas morons who didn't know to quit when they were ahead. Maybe I had thrown my last pitch, and it was a strike, and that was it.

## APRIL 2011:
## THE END IS THE BEGINNING IS THE END

| Followed | 🏠 ▶ 👥 ⏰ ⚙ |

| Comment 💬 | Followed 🚶 | Forward ➡ |

**Isaac Moss**

Dogsledded in Colorado—check

Declined meth in Kansas—check

Drove Patrick Swayze from Houston airport to hotel—check

Ran over an armadillo in New Orleans—check

Swam with manatees in Homosassa, Florida—check

Spent all my money—check

Hello Charleston, South Carolina! Do I know anyone here?

#fromseatoshiningsea

# ISAAC

## (50)

"NICE POST, LOSER," Cole tells me, scrolling his phone. We're at a bar on Folly Beach, looking at white sand and small olive green waves. Kids on summer break are whistling Nerf balls through the dusk, their final tosses of the day.

The bar has a small flat-screen hemmed into its upper corner. Sunday Night Baseball is on, the Nationals versus the Mets, Stephen Strasburg on the bump. Cole watches his one-time equal closely, fusses with a lime peel. He makes little noises, even chuckles after certain pitches, as though he has received a communication. There are creases at the corners of his eyes, like pine needles, when he sips his margarita. For the first time, I see what he'll look like when he's older.

"Excuse me? Do you happen to know where I might find a *San Francisco Chronicle*?" he asks. The bartender gives Cole a look that falls between curious and bothered.

"Try the hotel lobby, through those sliding doors," he says and motions with a tilt of his nose, but Cole is already off.

At the beginning of our trip, Cole said that once or twice he had told Dizzy she could play baseball for Seaside, that her arm was probably already better than all the boys. She hadn't rejected the idea, but hadn't reacted in any way that indicated she would follow through. And Cole never pushed the idea.

"You just couldn't with her," he said. "And you gotta respect that."

Since then, Cole wondered if she had given any more thought to baseball—if, in the after-school blunt huddle with the dim boys who held their pants by the crotch, she had ever thought of what it might be like to stand on the mound and feel in control?

Did she miss catch?

Had she picked up a ball since he'd gone?

"Probably she has no one to play with," Cole said, somewhere in Utah, his feet resting on the dash as we passed these giant plateaus.

"No one she's willing to show that side of herself to," he corrected.

We were on a Smashing Pumpkins stretch. Cole tolerated them, said they had substance, not like the other snivelers I tended to like. We'd listened to *Mellon Collie and the Infinite Sadness* from start to finish. Recording an album like that one was becoming a lost art, I felt. Albums once told stories. They had peaks and valleys, like Utah topography. Triumphs and devastations. Their sum was greater than their parts, but there seemed to be less room for that in this instant gratification age of MP3s.

I was driving, so Cole was on DJ, exhausting the Smashing Pumpkins catalog, hearing songs he'd never heard. He found their single from the *Batman Forever* soundtrack, "The End Is the Beginning Is the End."

"Delfino ain't vibing with catch," Cole said. "Majique and O'Shea, they have different preferences for recreation. Grayson has some arm irregularities. Mr. Antonini? Nah. I can't really see Dizzy playing catch with him. I could see him asking and her saying something like, 'Nah, I only did that to get outa vocab packets.' I'm not trying to convince myself I mattered in some special way to her, just saying what I think is real."

It seemed like Cole was beginning to feel, or worry, that he had not inspired Dizzy. That he'd left her with nothing. In our silent stretches on long country roads, I could tell it stung when she came to his mind, which happened more and more frequently. It was just like him to do this, use his magic wand

and manifest a dark cloud over himself.

So in what I felt to be a sad show of denial, he'd been checking the *San Francisco Chronicle* in each city we stopped in. Hotels, gas stations, wherever. He flipped through the *Sporting Green*, passed the Giants and A's and Warriors headlines, all the way to the back, where there were niche scores that only gambling degenerates paid attention to: boxing, sailing, World Series of Poker. But back there were local high school scores, and all the way from Vegas to Charleston, Cole had been looking for Dizzy's name in the high school box scores. Each day he'd found nothing. As of tonight, the high school baseball season is halfway done. If Dizzy's name hasn't appeared yet, come on, man, she never tried out for the team.

Cole returns with the *Chronicle*. He sits down with it and has a hell of a time folding it to the right section. It keeps bending like a wilted flower. He ruffles it, which gets it rigid for a moment, but then it loses its spine.

"This is a lost art," Cole says. "My dad dominates a newspaper. He can fold it in half twice, then inside out, all while on the can."

"Another margarita?" the bartender asks.

"Hang on," Cole says in the way of people so preoccupied they don't know how rude they sound.

Cole's eyes narrow. He pulls the paper close to his face, like he's in the darkroom watching a negative sharpen into fruition. He holds the paper in front of me with his finger pressed under a line of tiny type.

"What's that say?" he asks.

"LP Benson, one K, two runs, one-third of an inning."

"Read it again."

"Uh, LP Benson, with a strikeout and two runs?"

"Is this a dream?"

"It really says Benson."

"Her out was a strikeout!" he cries.

He stands, and the rest of the newspaper falls to the floor. He seems to be in search of someone to hug.

"So, margaritas?" the bartender asks.

"Oh yeah!"

Cole sounds innocent, *Leave It to Beaver*-ish.

"Calamari?" I loft.

"Why not! Hey, on me!"

Our bartender makes his mouth long and nods, as though we've just shown rare ingenuity.

"I'm keeping this," Cole says conspiratorially and starts to tear the newspaper. "So she took an L. So what? She can take an L. Better than me, better than anyone." He laughs again.

"Can you imagine?" he asks, but doesn't clarify, just leaves it there for the bartender and me. He kicks off his sandals and heads to the water. One last cool-off before we tie on a buzz and figure out where we'll sleep tonight. The pep in his step is something else. What I'm seeing now could be a seedling, set to bloom into a quirk with age, both annoying and endearing.

"Ask for aioli!" he calls.

The bartender gives me a knowing glance, which I take to mean—what would we be without our eccentric friends?

Cole steps into the ocean, puts his knee through a small wave, goes out until he's waist-deep. Then belly button. He leans back, and the water catches him.

The bartender sets down our margaritas, whose presentation both satisfies and disappoints in its plainness—plastic cups with ice and, in all likelihood, yellow Gatorade. The calamari, glistening in a wicker basket, comes next. The smell of grease and the sound of the surf make me understand the draw of life in these parts.

"Oh, and can we get that aioli?" I ask.

"Absolutely," the bartender says, more cordial than makes sense. Southern people have been nice. Probably because they don't know we're from San Francisco and haven't had a chance for their preconceptions to change their shape of us, like ours do when we hear syrup-thick drawls.

It reminds me that right now Cole and I have no home. It is here. It is everywhere. We share beds in hotels or drive through the night through small, unknown cities when we can't afford a room. I think about the man Cole taught with, Mr. Antonini, and his students, how their homes are a question mark.

I search the coast for Cole, from where the pier is to the set of condos. I see little neon swimsuits and boogie boards, but no Cole. I expand my search, out to where the dinghies are anchored, thinking maybe Cole shut his eyes and got ushered farther and farther out. No dice. Closer, I see a boy tossing a tennis ball and a chocolate lab chasing after it. And there, catching the ball with his palm, I see Cole. He pats the dog, who ignores the affection and sits expectant for the next toss. I watch the ball's back-and-forth. It's a lazy metronome, like the tide.

Cole calls the boy over, molds his little arm into a mannequin of proper technique. I watch the boy mirror, and Cole nods in approval. Then Cole rockets the ball away. Its flight is majestic, seems suspended in time. The dog returns, lays the ball at Cole's feet, and Cole sends it off again. If I were Cole, by now I'd want a shower. Rinse off the tight-skin feeling of dry salt. Rinse the stink. Instead I see him laughing at something the boy said with that goofy hiccup I used to hear more often. I sip the margarita, wipe its sweat on my pants leg, and pull up Followed on my phone, a post I remember seeing during Veritas's brief reign.

# Followed

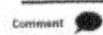

Comment 💬   Followed 🚶   Forward ➡️

**Daryl Seager**

Just watched the MLB Draft. Couldn't help but think about Cole Gallegos. Has anyone seen him, at least? He's just a Kid y'all.

**Comments:**

> **Jayce Limerick**
> He sat in front of me in Macro Policy. He just stopped showing up one day mid-semester.
>
> **Greg Calderon**
> Shows him right. What happens when u run frm ur problems.
>
> **Liz Bunting**
> Greg is right. If he was my son... I would be Ashamed!!!
>
> **Veritas Satire V**
> He's found his happy place
>
> **Daryl Seager**
> You mean He's DEAD?!

**Veritas Satire V**
No dumbass.

---

I type:

---

He's got margaritas and no money, which is to say, like you and me he's been better and he's been worse.

---

I hover my thumb over the Post button, the little rectangle, dopamine blue. The sun is at that point where there's barely any left, and you can actually watch it's yolky swan dance. My thumb moves away and instead holds Delete. The letters disappear one by one, until there's nothing, sweet nerve-racking nothing.

## ACKNOWLEDGMENTS

I'M GRATEFUL TO those who read this book in its various stages: Iris Garcia, Emmanuella Martin, Mark Panek, and Andy Slater. This book grew its identity from your discernment and generosity. Thanks to Matt Wilson for offering a lens into a world I didn't understand and still don't. Cheers to Bill Burleson and everyone at Flexible Press for believing in this story and being so fun and open to conversations along the way.

Most important though, for intersecting art with compassion, not just in spirit but with your checkbook. Mom and Dad, thanks for letting me bounce off the walls and bang loud drums; that had to have gotten old after a while.

The book doesn't exist without San Francisco: Thank you for raising me and others the way you do, including those who inspired this book.

And Kendall, without you I'd never have published a word or gotten a smog check or arrived anywhere on time.

## ABOUT THE AUTHOR

EMIL DEANDREIS HAS two prior books, *Beyond Folly* and *Hard to Grip*. His fiction has appeared in *StoryQuarterly*, *The Barcelona Review,* and more. He teaches English at College of San Mateo and lives in the Bay Area with his wife and son. www.emildeandreis.com

# MORE BOOKS BY EMIL DEANDREIS

### Hard to Grip: A Memoir of Youth, Baseball and Chronic Illness

In 2008, after a record-breaking career as a D1 college baseball player, Emil DeAndreis's life seemed set: He was twenty-three, in great shape, and had just been offered a contract to pitch professionally in Europe. Then his body fell apart. It started with elbow stiffness, then swelling in his wrist. Soon his fingers were too bloated to grip a baseball. *Hard to Grip* tells the story of a young man's body giving out when he needs it most.

### Beyond Folly

Welcome to the wonderful world of public education, as seen through the eyes of seasoned substitute teacher, Horton Hagardy. In *Beyond Folly*, we are on the front lines of the education system—in the trenches, so to speak, of what it feels like to face the everyday challenges of being a teacher on call. These thoughtful and insightful tales give the reader a behind-the-scenes peek into the life and mind of a substitute teacher, an isolated, underpaid, and underappreciated professional.

Made in the USA
Las Vegas, NV
03 December 2022